From the Files of

Madison Finn

Read all the books about Madison Finn!

Coming Soon!

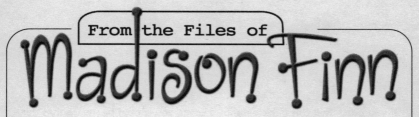

From the Files of

Madison Finn

To Have and to Hold

By Laura Dower

HYPERION
New York

Printed in the United States of America

First Edition
3 5 7 9 10 8 6 4

The main body of text of this book is set in 13-point Frutiger Roman.

ISBN 0-7868-1785-2

Visit www.madisonfinn.com

For Lois Gillooly,
super stepmother

From the Files of

Madison Finn

"You look nice tonight," Dad said, mumbling as he took a huge bite out of his bacon double cheese-burger. "I really like that outfit," he added.

Madison glanced down at her faded jeans and T-shirt that read *Go, Girl*.

"I look *nice*?" she said. "What planet are you on, Dad? I've had this ratty old T-shirt since fifth grade. And my jeans are ripped. You *hate* these pants."

"Well, is that a new hair clip?" Dad asked.

Usually, Dad was good at noticing the small, special details of Madison's appearance, but *a hair clip*?

"Oh, Dad!" Madison said, stuffing a fistful of fries into her mouth. She wiped ketchup from the corners of her mouth and stared down at the table.

"What's with you tonight? You're acting so goofy."

"I'm sorry," Dad said after a moment. "I'm a little nervous tonight, honey bear. I have something I need to say. Something important."

Madison rolled her eyes. "Dad, what could be so important that you can't just come right out and tell me?"

Dad took a long, deep breath. "It's something *very* important, Maddie. It affects you."

"Is it bad or good?" Madison asked.

Dad stared into her eyes. "Very good . . . I think."

"Does it have to do with your job?" Madison asked.

"Well, no . . ." Dad said.

"Does it have to do with me?" Madison asked.

"Maddie, I really don't want to play twenty questions," Dad said.

"Just tell me, Dad!"

Dad paused before he spoke.

"Stephanie and I have decided to get married," he said softly. He took a sip of his club soda.

Madison didn't blink. She stared straight ahead, mouth open, as if she'd just seen a UFO.

"Did you hear me?" Dad asked.

The room spun, and Madison felt as if she were floating above the booth where they were seated. She was suspended in midair over Dad, the French fries, and everything else in the restaurant. . . .

"Maddie, did you hear me?" Dad asked again.

"Yeah," Madison replied, crash-landing back at the table. "I heard you."

The waiter came over to pick up the dinner dishes and ask if either of them wanted dessert. Dad got a decaffeinated coffee. Madison ordered a giant slab of chocolate cake.

"Maddie, I understand if you feel weird about my getting remarried. This is a big deal for all of us. . . ."

"When is it going to happen?" Madison asked.

"We made plans with Stephanie's family for a small wedding on their ranch in a few weeks. . . ."

"A few weeks?" Madison cried.

"*Two* weeks, actually," Dad said.

"Two?" Madison said.

By now the chocolate cake had arrived. Madison dug into it and swallowed a big bite.

"Maddie, I know two weeks seems sudden, but Stephanie and I just don't see any reason to wait. We know this is what we want. We both have busy times coming up at work, so we figured it was a good idea to get the wedding taken care of now. And, as I said, it's not going to be a big wedding. Just family and a few very close friends. . . ."

Madison licked frosting off her fork.

"Are you okay?" Dad asked, looking ultracon-cerned. He raised his eyebrows. "Tell me whatever's on your mind. Please. Stephanie and I both want you to be happy about this."

"Can I have another piece of cake?" Madison

blurted out. Gorging on chocolate seemed like the best way to deal with the situation.

"Of course you can." Dad motioned to the waiter, who brought a new piece of cake immediately.

Madison didn't eat it. She pushed the plate off to the side. "I didn't think you'd really get married again. At least not so soon," she said to Dad. "Especially not after what happened with Mom . . ."

Dad reached across the table for Madison's hand. "I know it's sudden," he said. "But you really like Stephanie, don't you? And you know we're happy together. Isn't that what matters?"

"I guess," Madison said.

"Do we have your blessing?" Dad asked, smiling.

"Well . . ." Madison said.

"Naturally, we want you to be there. Stephanie and I already have big ideas. You will be a special part of the ceremony," Dad said. "We'll all fly to Texas together. . . ."

"Texas?" Madison cried.

"That's where the Wolfe family lives," Dad said. "They have a big ranch west of Houston, in a town called Bellville."

"Texas?" Madison said again. She felt her stomach flip-flop. "That's so far away. . . ."

"Not too far by plane. All the plans should come together this week. Since it's a low-key affair, I don't think you'll even have to pack much stuff," Dad said.

"Who else is going?" Madison asked.

"Not too many from my side of the family, except for Uncle Rick and Aunt Violet, who are flying down from Canada. Rick's my best man, of course."

Madison sighed. "That's it?"

"There may be a few more friends and family from our side. I have to call some people. But don't worry. You'll be surrounded by Stephanie's friends and family!" Dad gushed. "I can't wait to show everyone my little girl. . . ."

His voice trailed off. Madison looked down at the table. She hated it when he called her that. Didn't Dad know she was almost thirteen?

From the back of the restaurant, the jukebox started playing. The machine hummed and whirred before the loud chorus of Elvis Presley's "Love Me Tender" came on. Dad smiled again. He loved Elvis music—especially the mushy songs.

"Dad, didn't Stephanie almost get married before?" Madison asked.

Dad nodded. "Almost."

"What happened?" Madison asked.

"She called it off at the last moment."

"What if she does that again . . . with *you*?" Madison said.

"Oh, Maddie!" Dad cried. "How can you even say that? You know Stephanie! And she had real reasons for canceling that wedding. This is different."

"How do you know for sure?" Madison asked.

Dad's voice got low and serious. "Our wedding will happen, Maddie. I promise. I am in love with Stephanie. . . ."

"But you were in love with Mom once, too," Madison said.

"Yes, I was," Dad said solemnly. "I loved your mother very, very much."

"So why is this any different?" Madison asked. "I don't understand."

"Maddie, I know it hurts that your mom and I couldn't stay together. I don't know what else to say about the divorce. . . ."

For the last year, Madison had been recovering from the Big D. No matter how hard she tried to accept it, her gloomy feelings lingered.

Madison tapped with her fork on the table.

"Maddie," Dad said. He could tell she was thinking hard. "I don't know what you want me to say."

Madison sighed. "I don't know what you want me to say, either."

Dad cleared his throat as though he were thinking of a smart comeback, but he didn't speak. He just stared. Madison looked away.

The waiter came over with the dinner check, and Dad riffled through his wallet for cash. Madison quietly excused herself and headed for the ladies' room.

"I'll meet you out front," Dad said as she left.

By the time Madison returned, Dad had paid the

bill and was waiting by the front doors. Madison expected him to turn, open the outside door, and exit in silence.

But he didn't.

Instead, Dad blocked Madison's path and threw his arms around her.

"I love you so much," he said, squeezing her tighter than tight.

"Um . . . Dad?" Madison stammered. It was some hug. She couldn't move.

"I really want you to be okay with the wedding," Dad said, still squeezing. He sounded as though he were about to cry.

"Dad, I love you, too," Madison said. "But you can let go, now. People are looking. I—can't—breathe—"

"I just want you to be happy," Dad said, finally releasing her. "Like me. You know I love you, right? So does Stephanie. She thinks you're great—"

"You don't have to say all this," Madison interrupted.

"Yes, I do. Stephanie wants to be a big part of your life. She wants—"

"I don't need another mother," Madison said.

Dad stepped back and dropped his arms. "Maddie! Who said anything about *that*?" he cried.

"Can we talk about something else?" Madison asked. She walked a few paces in front of Dad as they headed for the parking lot.

7

"Maddie!" Dad said, struggling to catch up to her. "You're the most important person in my life."

"*Second* most," Madison corrected him. "Next to Stephanie, you mean."

"You are both important to me, for different reasons," Dad explained. "But you're my only daughter. . . ."

Madison kicked at some gravel in the parking lot. She usually liked the sound it made when her sneakers crunched over the top. But now, it didn't matter to her. Nothing seemed to matter.

"I'm tired, Dad," Madison said, getting into the car. "Can you take me home now? Please?"

Dad hopped into his car and turned on the ignition. They drove home in silence toward Blueberry Street. When Dad pulled up in front of the house, Madison leaned over to kiss him on the cheek before stepping out of the car.

"Thanks a lot for dinner," she said softly. "I didn't mean what I said."

"Can we talk about this some more?" Dad asked.

"I just . . . I feel . . . I want . . . I don't know, Dad," she sighed.

"Why don't I e-mail and call you later?" Dad said with a wink. "We'll figure this out. I promise."

Madison made a mental note of Dad's promises. Tonight he had dropped a mega-bombshell, but then, he had done everything he could to make things okay again. She had to give him credit for that.

Dad tooted the horn good-bye as Madison climbed the porch steps and opened the front door. Mom was waiting inside. Phin scooted over and started jumping up to give her some dog kisses.

"How was dinner?" Mom asked.

"Oh, Mom," Madison said. "I don't know how to tell you this."

Mom's face dropped. "What happened?"

Madison shook her head. "It's Dad," she said.

"Dad?" Mom asked. "What?"

Phinnie started to claw at Madison's sandals. He still had not gotten his proper hello. Madison leaned over and kissed her pug's head.

"Dad told me something awful tonight," Madison said. "He's getting married, Mom. Married!"

The hallway got quiet.

"Married?" Mom said. "Well, I knew it would happen sooner or later."

"You *knew*?" Madison cried.

"I knew your dad was serious about Stephanie. And he may have mentioned it once or twice. . . ."

"What?" Madison squealed. "You guys talked about this?"

Mom nodded. "I'm happy for him. For them."

Madison couldn't believe her mother was reacting this way.

"Happy?" Madison cried. "How can you be *happy*?"

"How can I be anything else?" asked Mom. She

wrapped her arm around Madison. "Let's sit down."

Madison collapsed onto the living room sofa, and Phinnie jumped into her lap and started licking her face.

"You can't be *that* surprised," Mom said. "You spend a lot of time with them. You know how close they are. Didn't you think one day Dad would—"

"Get married? Never! I mean, you just got divorced! Everything is happening too fast! The wedding is in two weeks. . . ."

"Two weeks?" Mom's jaw dropped. "Wow. That *is* fast. When your father makes up his mind to do something, he sure does it."

"And, of course, they want me to go," Madison said.

"Of course," Mom said, matter-of-factly.

"But I won't," Madison replied.

"Maddie . . ." Mom said, making a face.

"I won't go! I swear!" Madison said.

"Where is the wedding going to be held? With Stephanie's family in Texas?"

"How did you know that?" Madison asked.

"Lucky guess. So your dad will probably get you a plane ticket. . . ."

"Mom, I said I won't go!" Madison yelped.

"Rowrorooooo!" Phin yelped, too.

Mom bent down to quiet him.

Madison frowned. "Mom, I don't *want* Dad to get married again. I don't want things to change any more than they already have. Don't you understand? Are you even listening to me?"

Mom's face softened. She let go of Phinnie and took Madison into her arms. "Of course, I'm listening. . . ."

As they embraced, Phin started to growl. He didn't like being ignored. Phin nuzzled Madison and Mom with his cold, wet nose.

"Phinnie! Get down!" Madison said, half laughing and half crying.

Mom stepped away. "You'll be okay, honey bear," she said. "These things take time, that's all. You'll go to the wedding. Everything will work out. I promise."

Madison nodded, even though she was getting tired of hearing promises she wasn't sure her parents could keep. She said good night and headed upstairs for bed with Phinnie. Mom disappeared into her office to finish up some last-minute work.

As they reached the top of the stairs, Phin immediately jumped onto the bed and made a comfy spot for himself smack in the middle of Madison's stack of pillows. Madison went to her desk.

The orange laptop was waiting. It hummed as Madison powered it up.

Madison stared at a framed photograph on the filing cabinet by her desk that had been sitting there so long it had dust around the edges. She hadn't *really* looked at it for a long time.

It was a photograph that had been taken at Mom and Dad's wedding, almost fourteen years earlier. Mom was smiling. Dad was smiling. The sun was shining.

Madison leaned up, grabbed the picture, and shoved it into the top drawer of her desk.

The laptop screen flashed and she got online. It was a little after nine o'clock. She hoped that, since it was summertime, her friends would still be on the Internet.

Sure enough, Aimee Gillespie and Fiona Waters, Madison's two best friends in the world, were chatting online. Madison dropped in on them.

```
<Balletgrl>: Maddie! ur online? But
    I though u were w/ur Dad tonite
<MadFinn>: we just got home fm
    dinner
<Wetwinz>: So did I! my dad took us
    2 dinner at the Rainbow Diner
    awesome food and I saw Drew there
    2 with his rents
<Balletgrl>: how's Drew? what r u
    wearing to his pool party on
    Saturday?
<Wetwinz>: shorts & tshirt what
    about u?
<Balletgrl>: I got a new sundress!!
<MadFinn>: Hello? Can u pleez forget
    the party I have BIG NEWZ
```

```
<Balletgrl>: Spill it
<MadFinn>: my dad is getting
  married!!!
<Wetwinz>: 2 Stephanie?
<MadFinn>: duh of course who else?
<Balletgrl>: good one Fiona o:-\
<MadFinn>: The wedding is in 2 wks
  all the way in Texas and I have
  to be there!
<Balletgrl>: texas? KOOL!
<Wetwinz>: We stopped over once at
  Dallas airport
<MadFinn>: Hey this is sssssserious!
  Dad is getting married! WHAT AM I
  SUPPOSED TO DO?
<Wetwinz>: r u happy for him?
<Balletgrl>: sounds like fun. how do
  u feel?
```

Madison stared at the monitor. She didn't know how to feel. And she only had two weeks to figure it out.

Mr. and Mrs. Wallace Wolfe

Request the pleasure of your company

at the marriage of their daughter

Stephanie Mae

to

Jeffrey Peter Finn

on Saturday the Twentieth of July

at three o'clock in the afternoon

Wolfe Ranch

Bellville, Texas

Hoedown to follow –

Bring your lasso and spurs

Regrets Only

Chapter 2

From: MadFinn
To: Bigwheels
Subject: The Countdown Has Begun
Date: Fri 12 July 8:10 AM

Hey! U aren't appearing on my buddy list this A.M. But I know it's early and you prob aren't even up since ur halfway across the country and it's like 5 o'clock in the morning there so sorry.

Yesterday we got the invitations for my dad's wedding. I wanted to throw up. This whole week I thought I was getting used to the idea of him getting married but I guess I thought wrong. They were fancy invites too which is bizarre since Dad keeps saying only like fifteen or maybe thirty people max will be there. And BTW the guest list is mostly STEPHANIE'S family. There are hardly any Finns coming. Dad says it's no big deal but I think it is. Don't you?

At the end of the invite there's this line "regrets only" and I wanted to call him up and shout I HAVE REGRETS, DAD! DON'T DO IT!!! Yeah, but I won't.

I can't believe the wedding is now only ONE WEEK AWAY. I don't even know what I'm wearing. Mom wants to take me dress shopping this week.

I think I will wear all black. How's that sound? LOL.

I laughed at the jokes u sent me about stepmothers mainly because I can't believe Stephanie will be my stepmom.

My dad told me that there will be other kids my age at the wedding. I

wonder who? Stephanie has nieces and
nephews. Hmmmm. I wonder if any of
them are cute? (That is so perfect
--the worst day of my life so far
is coming up and all I can think
about is guys? LOL.)

Write again soon, okay? U know I
will.

Yours till the wedding bells,

Maddie

P.S.: I cannot believe ur parents
let u get another kitten! That is
so crazy. Does Pepper the new cat
like your cat Sparkles? I am so
glad u like animals as much as me.
I wish u could meet Phinnie!!!

After logging off, Madison trudged downstairs in
her Lisa Simpson T-shirt and slippers. The house was
steamy. Summer—along with other upcoming
events—was really heating up.

"Good morning, sunshine," Mom teased when
she saw Madison's gloomy expression.

"Can we put on the air conditioner, please?"
Madison asked.

"Just wait until you feel the temperatures in

Texas next week!" Mom said, laughing. "I imagine it must get up to ninety degrees or more in July."

Madison scrunched up her nose and stuck out her tongue. "Dad already told me to pack light. I can't believe I have to be sticky the whole time. It's like I'm being punished. . . ."

"Madison," Mom said seriously. "This week isn't about you. We've had this discussion a few times now. This is your dad and Stephanie's big day. You are a part of it, but . . ."

"Okay, okay," Madison said defensively. "I know, I know." She poured herself a glass of orange juice. "Where's Phin?" she asked.

"I think he went down to the basement so he could lie on the cool tile floor," Mom said.

"Maybe I'll go spend the day in the basement, too," Madison joked.

"Very funny," Mom said. "Actually, I have a big day planned. I need your help in the garden."

"Oh, Mom, it's so hot—"

"Maddie," Mom said, crossing her arms in front of her. "I have had just about enough of your complaining. You've been moping around for a week since your dad told you about the wedding."

"So?" Madison grumbled.

"Honey bear, I really need your help today," Mom said sweetly. "I have some weeding to do and I need to transplant some of the flowers from the side of the yard. Phinnie can hang outside with us."

"Okay! I'll help!" Madison said. She could tell there was no way out.

"I know this has been a hard week with the wedding planning and all," Mom said.

Madison realized that maybe she wasn't the only one who had to deal with Dad's big news. She stared hard at her mom.

"Is it hard for you, too?" Madison asked.

"What? The wedding?" Mom answered.

Madison nodded. "Aren't you jealous or something? I mean, Dad is getting married, and . . ."

"And what?" Mom asked.

"And you're not. . . ." Madison said with a gulp.

"Maddie," Mom said gently. "You have to understand. Your dad and I have separate lives now. We both love you and share our time with you, but otherwise, our lives are different. And right now, I have no plans to get married. I told you, I'm happy for your father. Believe me."

"Okay, okay, I believe you," Madison said, even though she didn't believe a single word Mom said.

Around ten o'clock that morning, Madison, Mom, and Phin headed into the garden with tools in hand. Mom carried a hoe in one hand and gloves and some small trowels in her portable green gardening bucket. Madison toted a handheld fan that sprayed water. She liked to aim it at Phin. The spray tickled his whiskers, and he did a little doggy dance.

Luckily, the weather wasn't as hot as Madison

had feared it would be. The sky looked clear, and there weren't many bugs flying around, either. Sometimes, Madison dreaded spending time in the garden, because she was paranoid about bees. Once, when she was younger, she'd disturbed a bees' nest by accident and sent the entire hive into a frenzy. That was one experience Madison wanted to forget.

Madison loved watching Mom dig in the garden dirt. Mom carefully checked the leaves and roots on her perennials.

"We should cut some of those and put them on the dining-room table," Mom said, pointing to an array of big, wide-eyed daisies in bright fuschia, gold, and orange (Madison's personal favorite). Mom had planted the flowers at the beginning of the summer, but they had only just exploded into colorful blooms.

Phinnie sniffed at Mom's feet. The yard was fenced in as a safety measure, but he always lingered close by whenever anyone was out planting or playing.

Mom shooed Phin away from some of her flowers, and he trotted over to Madison, who was down on her hands and knees digging new holes for transplanted perennials.

"Hello?"

Madison turned around to see her friend peering over the fence gate in the back.

"Aimee!" Madison cried, standing up.

"And Fiona!" another voice called out.

"Hey!" Madison replied.

"Can we come in?" Aimee asked.

Madison unlatched the garden gate. "Of course," she said. "I was just helping my mom plant."

"Your flowers look so nice," Fiona said, complimenting Madison's mom. "It's like a rainbow back here. Wow."

"Thank you, Fiona," Mom said as she stood up. "Can I get you girls something to drink?"

No one seemed very thirsty, so Mom invited everyone to help plant instead. Aimee and Fiona seemed eager to help.

"I wish I'd brought Blossom," Aimee said. "She could have played with Phinnie."

They glanced over at Phin, who was chasing a butterfly near a bush.

"Got your dress for the wedding yet?" Aimee asked.

"Almost," Madison replied. "Mom and I are shopping this week."

"I can't believe the wedding is *soooo* soon!" Fiona squealed.

"I guess I'm getting used to the idea," Madison admitted halfheartedly. "My dad calls me every day just to make sure I'm feeling good about it."

"Things will work out, Maddie," Aimee said, leaning in to give Madison a hug. Fiona joined in.

"I have an idea! Let's have lunch together. How does that sound, girls?" Mom asked.

Aimee and Fiona brightened. "Totally," they both said, almost in unison.

Madison giggled. Her BFFs could cheer her up.

The girls knelt down near Madison to help with some of the plantings. Madison showed them how to shake off the dirt and separate the roots.

Mom scurried inside to get the girls' sandwiches and Phin's kibble. As soon as she disappeared, Aimee grabbed Madison by the shoulders.

"Tell us everything about the wedding, Maddie!" Aimee said. "I didn't want to ask when your mom was here, but is Stephanie making you a flower girl, or what?"

"I don't think she's even having flower girls," Madison said.

"I was a flower girl at my cousin Darla's wedding," Fiona said. "Last summer in California. I had to wear this ugly, pink dress and take all the braids out of my hair. I hated it."

"I've never been in anyone's wedding!" Aimee complained. "What's so bad about being a flower girl anyway?"

Madison hung her head. "Being a flower girl is not as cool as being a bridesmaid," she said.

"Don't you have to be in high school to be a bridesmaid?" Fiona asked.

"I didn't know there were rules about all that stuff," Madison said.

Aimee plucked one of the flowers from the pile

of plants they were replanting and presented it to Madison on bended knee. "For the flower girl," she said, laughing.

Madison stuck the yellow bud in her ponytail. "Very funny, Aim."

"What are you getting Stephanie and your dad for a present?" Fiona asked.

Madison's face went blank. "A present?"

Aimee rolled her eyes. "Maddie! It's a wedding. How could you forget that you need a wedding gift?"

"I only have a little money saved from baby-sitting," Madison said. "I can't afford a real gift."

"There's a major sale at the Far Hills Shoppes next weekend," Aimee said.

"But I'm leaving for Texas before then," Madison said.

"Why don't you *make* something?" Fiona suggested.

"Like what?" Madison asked.

"Make one of your cool collages," Fiona said. "Write something on it, like a poem. You're good at that."

"That's a killer idea!" Aimee cheered. She danced around a little more and picked up another one of the blooms from the lawn. "You could put flowers in your collage, too!"

Madison thought about the suggestion. And the

longer she thought, the more she liked it. A collage was a perfect way to tell Dad and Stephanie her feelings about them, the wedding, and the future.

"Lunch is served!" Mom announced, reappearing outside the house. She carried a tray of sandwiches, and some chips and juice. Phin trotted out behind her, a rawhide doggy bone in his jaws.

Aimee, Fiona, and Madison gathered to eat together under a maple tree in the backyard. After eating the sandwiches, they nibbled on some of Mom's oatmeal-cookie crisps. Then they finished the planting and hosed down their handiwork. Transplanted flowers needed an extra-good soaking, Mom said.

It was nearly six o'clock by the time Aimee and Fiona left. The sun was still shining, and no one seemed tired. It had been a productive—and supportive—afternoon for Madison and her friends.

After saying goodbye, Madison headed inside to wash up. She wanted to check her e-mail, too. Sure enough, the mailbox was blinking. Her keypal had written back.

```
From: Bigwheels
To: MadFinn
Subject: Re: The Countdown Has Begun
Date: Fri 12 July 4:36 PM
Sorry I wasn't home when u wrote
b4, I wish we could have chatted
```

online! I was babysitting my stupid
brother and sister who r driving me
bananas. Mom thinks I should watch
them all summer long. Can u believe
that? But she sez she'll pay me.
That's cool.

Is ur Dad's wedding really in one
week??? R u really traveling all
the way to Texas? I know u said ur
having 2nd thoughts but it sounds
exciting 2 me. Don't forget 2 bring
ur laptop so u can write to me the
whole time ur there, ok?

I was thinking u should get a long
dress in a pale color like sherbet
or something. Does that sound weird?
I saw one in the Boop-Dee-Doop cata-
log that I loved. You could wear it
with their platforms--the ones with
the crossover straps by the toe.

All ur emails about weddings make me
wish that I were in love too. I
wish I was still talking 2 Reggie.
He's away now for the whole summer.
I've never really been in love. Have
u seen Hart lately? What did he say
when u told him you were going to a
wedding?

GTG. My sister is pulling on me to go play in the sprinklers. Please WBS. Isn't tomorrow that big pool party u told me about? HAGT!!!

Yours till the swim suits,

Bigwheels aka Vicki

Madison hit SAVE so she could reread Bigwheels's e-mail again later.

Then she ducked into her closet to plan an outfit for Drew's pool party.

Chapter 3

Madison tugged at her blue cargo Capri pants. She'd loved them in the store and hanging in her closet, but now she wasn't sure if they made her waist look too pudgy.

"Maddie! Aimee and Fiona are waiting down-stairs!" Mom called up to Madison's bedroom.

Drat!

The pants would have to stay, Madison thought with panic, as she threw other piles of unfolded clothing and rejected outfits back into the closet. She quickly decided on a pale yellow top to match the pants and yanked it on over her one-piece bathing suit. Then Madison shoved a towel and flip-flops into her bag, along with the latest copy of *Star Beat* magazine. She was dying to show Aimee and

Fiona the cover article about the twenty-five hottest teen stars in Hollywood.

Phin followed Madison downstairs.

"Call you later, okay, Mom?" Madison said as she whisked past her mother and leaned over to kiss Phin good-bye.

"Don't be too late! You are having supper with your father this evening!" Mom reminded her.

Madison nodded. Since the wedding planning had kicked into high gear, Dad had been checking in daily and dropping by for more regular visits. He wanted to make sure that Madison was cool with everything that was happening. On this particular night, he'd made plans to have Madison join him and Stephanie for dinner.

"Maddie! Sorry we're late. It was my fault!" Fiona called out from the window of Mrs. Gillespie's car as Madison skipped down the driveway.

"Love those pants!" Aimee cried as she pushed open the minivan door so that Madison could climb inside.

Madison beamed. She had made the right fashion choice.

Aimee wore a flowered halter top and peasant-style skirt with fringes and appliquéd flowers along the bottom.

"You're so dressed up, Aim," Madison said.

Aimee just shrugged. "Aw, this old thing!" she joked.

Madison guessed Aimee's outfit was carefully planned. Aimee wanted to look good for her crush, Ben Buckley, who she hoped would also be at the pool party.

Fiona was dressed casually. She wore faded jeans shorts and a T-shirt that read *Far Hills Girls' Soccer*. Even when she wasn't headed for team practice, Fiona liked announcing her love of the sport.

"I have to borrow that shirt sometime," Fiona said, pointing to Madison.

The drive to Drew's house passed quickly; Aimee, Fiona, and Madison talked about clothes, and Madison pulled out her copy of *Star Beat* to show her friends. After about ten minutes, Mrs. Gillespie called out from the front seat. "Okay, troops, we're heeeeere!" and the girls grabbed their stuff and piled out of the car.

The Maxwell house wasn't really a house at all. It was a mansion, with bushes trimmed into animal shapes, sculpture on the front lawn, and a fountain in the middle of the driveway.

Drew sat on the steps waiting for his guests to arrive. Next to him, playing on a Gameboy, was Walter "Egg" Diaz, one of Madison's best guy friends and Fiona's "sort-of" boyfriend. As soon as Egg caught a glimpse of Fiona, he ditched the Gameboy, stashing it in his pocket, and ran over to say hello. Drew came with him.

"Hey, Fee," Egg said, walking right up to Fiona.

He had decided on a new nickname for her. That way, he could have a special name for her that was all his own.

"Hey, Walter," Fiona replied. She had the distinction of being the only person other than Egg's parents who called him by his real name.

Fiona twirled one of her braids between her fingers.

"Okay, you guys," Aimee cried. "Enough! You're making me nauseous."

Egg ignored Aimee. Madison just giggled. These days, she was used to super sappy behavior, especially since Dad and Stephanie were acting lovey-dovey all the time, now that they were getting married.

The friends wandered through the front entryway and into the Maxwell foyer through the living rooms (there were two), then through two giant sliding doors and onto the backyard patio. The place was packed. Clusters of kids and adults mingled around the lawn.

"Cool, huh?" Drew said, pointing to a row of golden torches. "Mom got them shipped here from Samoa or something."

"Come on!" Aimee said. "You can get those at the home decorating store in downtown Far Hills for five bucks!"

"Really?" Drew said. "Well, they're cool, anyhow." He didn't seem to care where they had come from.

Madison laughed. "Drew, your family has parties like no one else ever in the history of parties, I swear."

The Maxwell parties included friends, friends of friends, and parents of friends. Each event had its own theme. On this occasion, Mrs. Maxwell's caterer had assembled a tropical-drinks bar, with smoothies for all age groups. Hawaiian music was piped in, and dozens of torches decorated the edges of the pool and yard.

As they walked around, Fiona and Egg paired off, and Aimee vanished to go find Ben Buckley. Madison wanted to find Hart, but he wasn't around, so she hung out on the edge of the group with Drew.

"So when's your dad's big wedding?" Drew asked. Even though it was summer, all of Madison's friends found ways to catch the latest gossip. Madison's upcoming trip to Texas was on everyone's radar.

"The wedding is this weekend," Madison said. "But I don't want to go."

"How come?" Drew asked.

"Simple," Madison said. "I don't want Dad to get married."

"Yeah," Drew nodded. "I know what you mean. My stepbrother, Ben, always told me funny stories about how weird it was when my dad got remarried. He hated my mom. The whole stepfamily thing is pretty complicated. But you'll get used to it. We did."

"Do you think so?" Madison asked. "Because, right now, the idea of having a stepmother is freaking me out."

"But isn't your dad's girlfriend nice?" Drew asked.

"Yeah," Madison grumbled. "That's what makes it so annoying."

"Parents say they care about our opinions and all that. But they still do what they want," Drew said simply.

"I know," Madison said.

"It'll be cool," Drew said, patting Madison on the back. He smiled, and Madison felt her stomach do a little flip. She wasn't sure why. Drew didn't usually touch Madison on the back—or anywhere. She caught her breath and shook off the feeling. This was Drew, after all, not Hart! And even though the two boys were cousins, Drew was definitely not someone Madison saw herself crushing on.

Never. Ever.

"Who else is here?" Madison asked, trying to change the subject. "I recognize some of the people from the last barbecue."

Drew grinned. "Yeah, Mom invited the whole planet, of course. There's someone special I want you to meet."

Madison grinned. Maybe Drew was about to introduce her to *another* cute cousin of his? She liked that idea.

"Wait until you see the karaoke setup my parents bought," Drew said. "We have the system hooked up to the main stereo system, with speakers out here by the pool. It's got excellent sound. We can do solos, duets, and group numbers."

Madison was always flabbergasted by the way Drew was able to have games and electronics and whatever else he wanted—and still act like a normal kid. He was a good friend, she told herself as they stood there on the lawn together. She didn't always give him enough credit.

"There you are!" a voice yelled from across the lawn.

A girl with short, black hair ran toward Drew and Madison, arms flailing. She wore a pale yellow sundress and little butterfly barrettes in her hair.

"Drew! Drew!" the girl called out breathlessly.

Madison squinted at the girl. She'd never seen her before.

"I've been looking for you," the girl continued. "I was helping your dad set up the karaoke machine. When do you want to start it up?"

"Whenever," Drew said with a big smile. "Thanks for helping."

Madison rocked from foot to foot, watching Drew, watching the girl, watching Drew.

"Maddie, this is Elaine Minami," Drew said, finally. "Do you know her? Oh, well, I guess you wouldn't. She's our neighbor up the street."

Madison knew that Drew was one of the only kids in his neighborhood who went to the public junior high. The rich kids who lived nearby went to private schools or even to boarding schools outside Far Hills.

"Hiya!" Elaine said. She had a voice like a cartoon mouse, Madison thought. Elaine didn't talk. She squeaked.

Drew seemed to like it, though.

"It's *soooo* great to meet all of Drew's friends from school," Elaine said. She couldn't stop moving when she talked.

"Nice to meet you, too," Madison said.

"Elaine, this is Maddie . . . er . . . Madison," Drew said.

"Hey, Finnster!"

From behind Madison, the familiar sound of Hart's voice sent a thrill up her spine. She'd looked for him everywhere, and now he was finally here.

Normally, she would have spun around and glanced to see what Hart was wearing, or how his soft, brown hair looked. But this time, she didn't. Right now, all Madison could focus on was Elaine and Drew.

"Hiya, Hart!" Elaine chirped.

Madison couldn't believe it. Elaine knew him, too? Within minutes, it seemed as if all the boys at the party were gravitating toward the section of the yard where Madison was standing with Drew, Hart, and Elaine. And Elaine knew all of them—including Fiona's brother, Chet, and Madison's good guy friend Dan Ginsburg.

How was that possible?

Aimee sidled up to Madison. "What's up over here?" she asked. "Who's she?" Aimee pointed to Elaine.

Madison explained; Aimee rolled her eyes.

"She probably knows everyone because she's always hanging out here when the guys come over to Drew's. . . ." Aimee said with a groan. "Guys are so predictable. Look at them, like a bunch of flies or something. . . ."

Madison chuckled. "Yeah," she agreed.

"So, what?" Aimee continued. "Is she going out with Drew or what? I cannot believe he has a girlfriend!"

"I can't tell," Madison said, trying to figure out whether they were a couple or not. "She seems nice."

"She isn't very pretty," Aimee said.

Madison fake-punched her BFF in the shoulder. "Don't say that!"

Aimee took it back immediately. "Well, it doesn't matter, anyway. What do we care who Drew likes? I mean, I thought he liked you for a while, but everyone changes."

Madison frowned. "Yeah," she said.

"I didn't find Ben inside or by the pool or anywhere," Aimee said, distractedly.

Madison kept staring over at Elaine, who seemed poised and happy. Why did Madison feel so much the opposite?

"Aimee! Maddie!" Fiona's voice trilled from across the yard. She came running over, with Egg in tow. "What is everyone doing over here?" Fiona asked.

"Look," Aimee said, nodding in Drew's direction.

Madison always thought it was funny that Drew could be such a "follower" at school, but Mr. Party on days like this.

"This is *so* not a kid's party," Aimee grumbled. "I mean, it's fun to come here and have music and swimming and games, but . . ."

Madison knew Aimee was right. People none of them knew strolled around in caftans and bikinis, carrying little glasses of pink-and-orange smoothies topped off with mini-umbrellas and chunks of pineapple. Mrs. Maxwell breezed from guest to guest, passing out leis.

"I don't see you-know-who anywhere," Fiona said with a raised eyebrow.

Madison knew exactly who Fiona was talking about.

Fiona was talking about Poison Ivy Daly, public enemy number one at Far Hills Junior High, and a permanent and annoying fixture in Madison's life.

"I heard she went away to the beach," Aimee said.

36

"Whew," Madison said. "I hope it was a faraway beach. Did I tell you what happened when I ran into her in our neighborhood last month?"

"You saw her in *our* neighborhood?" Fiona asked.

"I think she was visiting Rose Thorn," Madison grumbled. "I was walking Phinnie, and Ivy totally passed by me. She didn't even say hello. None of the drones did, either. I heard them *laughing* at me."

"Are you really surprised?" Aimee said.

"I wish I knew how to put a hex on Poison Ivy," Madison said.

"You don't really mean that!" Fiona said.

Madison smiled. "Oh, yes, I do. I'm sick of her and her perfect clothes and hair and I wish she would just . . . evaporate!"

The three BFFs laughed.

All at once, Aimee's face lit up. "Look! Over there! I think that's Ben! Over by that torch!" She dashed away.

"Aim?" Madison said to her departing friend's back.

Fiona laughed, her voice mocking Aimee's tone. *"Oh, Ben! Ooooh! Over by that torch!"*

"I didn't know she liked him that much," Madison said.

"I just can't believe she acts that way around a boy. . . ." Fiona said, still laughing.

Madison laughed, too. "What are you talking about, *Fee*?" she said, teasing her friend using Egg's new nickname for her.

Fiona blushed. "I don't act that way around Egg, do I?" she asked self-consciously.

Madison threw her arm around Fiona's shoulder. "Nah, I was only kidding," she said.

"How embarrassing," Fiona said. "My dad told me that I act different whenever Egg comes over to hang with Chet. Do you think that's true?"

"Your dad said that?" Madison said.

"Is that weird?" Fiona said with a shrug. "Daddy's always asking me and Chet stuff about our friends—especially guy friends. He quizzes me all the time. I think he worries too much."

"Yeah, my dad worries a lot, too," Madison said.

"How's your dad doing with the wedding?" Fiona replied. "Freaked out?"

Madison nodded. "Well, Dad's always a little freaked out," she said jokingly. "But I'm having dinner with him and Stephanie tonight."

"That will be fun," Fiona said. "Right?"

Madison shrugged. "Yeah, like going to the dentist."

Fiona giggled. "Quit stressing about the wedding," she said. "We promise we'll help you get through it."

Madison gave Fiona a big hug. They walked over to a throng of partygoers setting up for karaoke.

Drew stood on a chair telling people where to go and what to do. Elaine helped out by handing out song lists to the crowd.

Madison ended up doing a karaoke song with Aimee, Fiona, and Elaine. They sang "Summer Nights" from *Grease* along with Drew, Egg, Chet, and Dan. Hart sat that one out, claiming a sudden attack of laryngitis.

Mrs. Gillespie didn't come back to pick the girls up until after five. Madison worried that she wouldn't have time to get home and get dressed for her dinner with Dad and Stephanie.

But she had plenty of time.

She even had *extra* time, to open a new file.

 Pairs

Rude Awakening: Usually it's the bride and groom who get nervous before a wedding. How come <u>I'm</u> the one getting cold feet?

All the times Dad and Stephanie hung out with me <u>before</u> getting engaged, I was okay with it. But sooner than soon the two of them will be hitched forever and I'm NOT okay with that. Why is everyone pairing off around me? I'm not a third wheel. I'm more like a flat tire.

That's even how I felt today at Drew's pool party. Fiona paired off with Egg. Aimee paired off with Ben. Even Drew paired off with that girl Elaine. (P.S. where did she come from? Didn't Aimee say that Drew liked _me_?)

The only good thing about the party was that I didn't have to see Poison Ivy. She's always hanging all over Hart. And even though he claims they're only friends, it seems like more to me! She acts like he belongs to her. Ugh.

In a world of pairs, I'm living solo.

Chapter 4

Madison clutched her dinner napkin tightly under the table.

Dad was sitting on the banquette, holding Stephanie's shoulder. Her brown hair shimmered in the candlelight.

It was dinner for two. Except that Madison was there, too.

Stephanie turned and bent down to reach her bag. She pulled out a small, wrapped package.

"It's for you," she said, sliding it across the white tablecloth toward Madison.

"Me?" Madison asked, taking the package in her hands. She peeled off one corner of tape and lifted out a small, dark-green, leather-bound book.

"I had it monogrammed," Stephanie said. She pointed to the front cover. There, in the corner, were Madison's initials in beautiful script: MFF.

"What's it for?" Madison asked, still a little bewildered about the gift. She looked down at the title: *Love Poems for the Ages.*

"What's it for? Is that all you have to say, Maddie?" Dad asked.

"Oh," Madison said. "I'm sorry. Thank you, Stephanie."

"It's actually a special gift for the wedding," Stephanie explained. "You'll see that one of the pages has been marked. That's a sonnet your father and I picked out for the wedding. It's by William Shakespeare. We'd like you to read it at the ceremony."

Madison's heart began to thump.

"You want me to read a poem by Shakespeare?" Madison said.

Stephanie grinned. "I know that you'll do an excellent job."

"I'm not really good in front of large groups," Madison mumbled. "I get kind of nervous. . . . and sometimes I get all sweaty and . . ."

Madison bowed her head, embarrassed. Even though the sweaty part was true. . . . what had she said *that* for? It sounded gross.

"Oh, honey bear!" Dad chimed in. "You'll be the best. I know it."

"Come on, open the book," Stephanie said.

Madison cracked the spine as she opened the front cover. The leather smelled new. On the inside front page, Madison saw some handwritten words:

For Madison Francesca
Bright light, shining star—
We love you.
Dad and Stephanie

She glanced up at Stephanie, whose eyes looked a little wet. It was if everything had slowed down to slow motion with fuzzy filters.

"Maddie," Stephanie said. "I am so happy to be a part of your life."

Madison looked over at Dad, but his eyes had also glazed over.

What was going on here? She felt as though she'd been shoved into the center of some late-night, T.V. melodrama.

This was too much of a love-fest even for Madison. Her stomach heaved. It felt hot inside the restaurant, and she was reeling from the smell of garlic at the next table. Of course, Madison wanted to be nice and polite about the poetry book Stephanie and Dad had given to her, but, at the same time, she wanted to run away.

Meanwhile, Dad and Stephanie intertwined their arms and leaned in toward Madison. Dad kissed

Stephanie's cheek, and she let out a little sigh. It was enough PDA (Public Display of Affection) to make *anyone* sick to her stomach, especially Madison.

Luckily, the waiter showed up with appetizers. Madison used the plates of salad as an excuse to set the leather-bound poetry book aside—at least for the moment. She didn't want to get any salad dressing on it.

"Maddie, in addition to the poem, I wanted to ask you if you would . . . oh . . . How do I say this? Jeff, help me out here," Stephanie stammered. She couldn't spit out the words she needed most of all.

Dad smiled at his fiancée. "What Stephanie is trying to say, Maddie, is will you stand up for her at the wedding?"

Madison nodded. "I know, I just said I would stand up for her. I'll read the poem. I assumed that I would be standing up to do it. . . ."

"Oh, no!" Stephanie gasped, giggling a little in response. "I mean 'stand up' for me as a brides-maid—as my junior maid of honor, actually."

Madison could barely breathe. No words came out of her mouth.

"Maid of honor?" she finally said.

"My sister Wanda will be my matron of honor, but I thought it would be nice to have you right up there with us, too," Stephanie added. "Jeff has his brother Rick as his best man, plus my nephew as junior best man."

"Don't I have to be older to stand up for you at the wedding?" Madison asked, her voice shaking a little bit. "I'm only in junior high, remember? I'm supposed to be a flower girl, aren't I?"

"Actually, I think people can plan their weddings any way they want," Dad said.

"And this is how we want it," Stephanie said.

Madison felt a surge of emotion from her belly right up to her neck. She had more than a lump in her throat now. This was a brick.

"Just how many bridesmaids are you having?" Madison asked.

Stephanie turned to Dad. "How many is it, hon?" she asked him. "Six?"

Dad rolled his eyes. "Some small wedding," he said with a little cough.

"Let me see. . . . I think there are fifteen girls and guys in the wedding party," Stephanie explained. "That includes four bridesmaids, a junior maid of honor, a maid of honor, four groomsmen, a best man, and a junior best man. Plus two flower girls and a ring bearer."

Madison's head was spinning.

Fifteen?

The original number of guests—according to Dad—had been only fifteen or so.

"Wait. Stephanie, I'm confused." Madison said. "I thought you and Dad said this was a small wedding?"

45

Dad's face brightened up. "See, Stephanie? My point exactly!" he said.

Stephanie shushed him. "Don't start again, Jeff," she said sweetly." It really isn't that many people, Maddie. My mother just got a little carried away with the guest list."

"A *little* carried away?" Dad teased. "Why don't you tell Maddie how many people are on the guest list now?"

"Well, the party started at thirty or so guests. But now I'd say it's up to a hundred. My mother likes to overdo it. Not to worry, though. I promise it won't be much bigger. Really. This should be it."

"A hundred people? Wow. Just how big is your house?" Madison asked.

Dad grinned. "Big."

"Oh, Jeff," Stephanie said, hitting him lightly on the arm. "He's exaggerating. The house is not that big. . . ."

"Yeah, but the ranch is," Dad said.

"Well, you have friends coming, too," Stephanie insisted.

"Yeah," Dad replied. "Maybe five or six. What percentage is that of the total number, Stephanie?"

She rolled her eyes and crossed her arms.

Madison stood back and watched as Dad and Stephanie bounced comments off each other as if they had been tossing a ball back and forth.

"Well, I don't think having a lot of family is that

bad. There always will be things to do and people to do them with," Stephanie said. "Don't you agree, Jeff?"

Stephanie nudged him with her elbow.

"Oh, yeah," Dad said, winking at Madison.

"Since you won't have any cousins from your side of the family there, Maddie, you can spend time with some of my nieces and nephews who are just your age," Stephanie went on. "Doesn't that sound like fun?"

Madison pasted on a smile. "Fun," she repeated. "What am I supposed to wear? I didn't get a dress yet."

"Since it's such a rush, there are no specific dress requirements for the bridesmaids or maids of honor. I know your mother was planning to take you shopping. . . ." Stephanie said.

Madison wrinkled her nose. How did Stephanie know about *that*?

Madison looked over at Dad.

"Your mother called me to find out if there was a color theme or anything," Dad said, in response to Madison's glare. "What do I know about color themes? So I asked her to speak to Stephanie directly."

Madison pinched her finger hard to keep from yelping. How could Mom have spoken to Dad's girlfriend and not said anything about it?

Stephanie spent the rest of the dinner telling

Madison more details about how the ranch was being decorated and how it still really was just going to be a very simple ceremony with the closest friends and family. According to Stephanie, the day before the wedding would be relatively quiet and easy. Madison would have a chance to see some of Texas, go swimming, and just hang out at the hotel or the ranch.

It sounded okay, Madison decided, although she didn't know what it would be like to spend so much time with such a gigantic family. As an only child, Madison hardly ever spent holidays or major events with a kid her own age.

This would be way different.

"Hey, Maddie, when you get the dress, just don't pick out some super short outfit with lots of Big Bird feathers," Dad cracked at the end of the meal.

Madison grinned. "Okay, Dad," she shot back. "I guess I'll return the yellow boa and my leather miniskirt."

Stephanie chuckled and took a sip of wine. "Whew! I can't believe the wedding is only days away."

"Me neither, sweetheart," Dad said, leaning in to kiss Stephanie's cheek again. She cooed at him.

Once again, Madison was beamed out of the conversation and into the peanut gallery.

The love-fest was back.

* * *

"Did you have a good dinner?" Mom asked when Madison bounced through the front door after being dropped off by Dad and Stephanie.

Madison kicked off her sandals. "You didn't tell me that you had talked to her, Mom!" she said.

"Talked to whom? Stephanie?" Mom said.

Madison nodded. "Uh-huh. You actually talked to her on the phone, like, person to person?"

"What's the big deal?" Mom asked. "She was telling me about her wedding palette."

"What's that?" Madison asked.

"The colors of her ceremony. She and Dad aren't sticking to any color combinations. So, you can pick out whatever color dress you like, as long as it's a pale color. That was all she asked."

"Pale?" Madison cried. "But I look yucky in pale colors. *I'm* pale!"

"No," Mom said reassuringly. "You look beautiful in anything you wear, honey bear."

"We'll never find the right dress. I know it," Madison said.

Phinnie toddled over with a yawn. He'd been sleeping when Madison had come back from dinner.

"Rooooooooooohhhhhhhhhhhhhrrrrrrrrr!" Phin yawned again.

"Do you think we'll find the perfect pale dress?" Madison asked the dog.

Mom squeezed Madison by the shoulders. "Young lady," she said in a mock-stern voice. "If you don't quit this negative stuff, I'm going to send you to your room with no supper."

Madison laughed. "I already ate, Mom. Some threat."

"Well, I stink at threats," Mom said, laughing a little herself. "Now, will you please just be nice about the wedding once and for all? Please?"

"Okay, okay," Madison said. "I will. I promise."

Madison realized that she was making a promise that she might not be able to keep. But she made it anyway.

The clock in the kitchen read nine-twenty. It was later than Madison had thought. After saying good night to Mom, she skipped upstairs with Phin at her heels. She immediately yanked off her dinner outfit and changed into her pajama bottoms and a tank top. It was cooler in the house than it had been all week. Mom had finally turned on the air conditioner.

Madison booted up her laptop.

The screen blinked on with a special photograph of a leaping leopard that slowly faded into a splotchy red snake. Earlier in the summer, Egg had lent Madison a disk containing animal images, and she had loaded her computer with his entire collection, from bugs to beasts. Photos of endangered species were her personal favorites.

Her e-mail was slow to open. When it finally did, the mailbox was empty.

"Aw, Phin," Madison groaned. "Nobody loves us."

Just then, an Insta-Message appeared at the corner of Madison's screen. Aimee and Fiona were online and they wanted to chat. The three BFFs went into a private chat room called SMRFRDS, an acronym for summer friends.

```
<Balletgrl>: MAdDIE!
<MadFinn>: hey guys
<Wetwinz>: we just got back from
    Freeze Palace u should have been
    there
<MadFinn>: y???
<Balletgrl>: drew came w/Elaine
    ooooooh
<MadFinn>: so? They live next door
    maybe they just rode their bikes
    there or something
<Wetwinz>: LOL
<Balletgrl>: hart was wundering
    where u were
<Wetwinz>: and dan too HA HA
<MadFinn>: what? Hart?
<Wetwinz>: love connection LOL
<MadFinn>: what r u talking about?
<Balletgrl>: maddie!!! we're just
    kidding
<MadFinn>: VVF
<Wetwinz>: tee hee
<MadFinn>: y do u always tease me
    like that?!
<Balletgrl>: b/c we miss yooooooo!
```

```
<MadFinn>: WAM u just saw meeeeee
<Wetwinz>: yeah but you've been so
   busy w/ur dad & the wedding it
   feels like we havent seen u as
   much and now ur going away this
   weekend boo hoo
<MadFinn>: I'll be back in 3dayz
<Balletgrl>: BTW how was STEPMOM LOL
<MadFinn>: NC
<Balletgrl>: hey tonite on cable
   there is this excellent movie
   let's watch it together
<MadFinn>: I'm already in my PJs
<Balletgrl>: I don't mean watch it
   together @ the same house DUH
   watch it together @ the same time
<MadFinn>: oops DOUBLE DUH
<Wetwinz>: aim is the movie called
   KISS UP or something?
<MadFinn>: so cheezy
<Wetwinz>: oh GTG chet wants online
   now
<Balletgrl>: brothers r annoying
<MadFinn>: TTYT
<Wetwinz>: l8r
<Balletgrl>: *poof*
```

Madison smiled as she went *poof*, even though she didn't really want to say good-bye to her friends. She complained, but secretly Madison didn't always mind being teased.

If only Aimee and Fiona knew about her real feelings for Hart.

After leaving the chat area, Madison reopened her files and typed in a new heading.

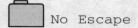 No Escape

According to my sources (um, that would be Dad and Stephanie) this is no big wedding. Yeah right. No one has fifteen people in a bridal party and asks some 12-year-old (um, that would be me) to stand up for them when they have just about a million older friends and family who could do the same thing. Do they?

I'm so nervous about traveling all the way to Texas to spend three days with a bunch of people I've never met before. And the worst part is now Mom says I can't bring Phin. I didn't think I would be able to, because we're staying in a hotel and everything, but I hoped.

Sometime during dinner tonight, after Stephanie gave me the leather book of poems (that I still have not really read and don't know when I will), I started thinking about all the stuff I still need to do before we got to Texas. And not just buying a dress. I have to get shoes, too! Do I get strappy sandals or flats or what?

I haven't even started to think about the collage I'm making for a wedding gift. It has to be stellar, not just some ordinary words pasted down on a piece of paper. And I should probably start working on my poem for it first, but I have no clue what to write about. ARRGGGH!

I do know one thing. Unlike Stephanie, I won't get all mushy and weepy and say a bunch of dorky serious stuff about love. And Dad just lets her be that way! I thought it was nice at first but it is really very embarrassing.

Rude Awakening: On the keyboard of life, I think I need to keep one finger on the escape key.

This is going to be a loooooong week.

Poem for Dad and Stephanie

Your wedding is a ~~special great~~
~~wonderful~~ special (ACK!!) day
And you will be feeling good
   in every way
The sun is shining bright on your
   ~~heads~~ FACES
And there is no one who can take
   your places
(No one?)
~~How am I supposed to deal when~~
~~I don't know what I feel?~~
Thank u for making me a part of
the day (change this word)
OH I DON'T KNOW WHAT TO SAY!!!!!!

BLAH!

Chapter 5

Mom couldn't find a parking space anywhere at the Far Hill Shoppes. Part of the lot and garage were under construction.

"I can't believe the mall is this crowded! It's Monday!" Mom groaned.

Madison sulked in the front seat, too. She wasn't in the mood to buy a dumb wedding dress, even if she was a junior maid of honor.

They finally found a place to pull in, but it meant walking half a mile back to the stores they needed to visit. The sky was slate gray, threatening rain and maybe thunder. Madison dragged her grumpy self into the air-conditioned mall behind Mom. They stopped at the Coffee Counter, where Mom bought an iced latte.

Madison scanned the enormous mall crowd to see if anyone she knew was there. Usually, a visit to the downtown shops meant bumping into half her class from FHJH, but not today. Madison guessed a lot of kids were hanging by the pool or traveling somewhere for summer vacation by then.

"There's the dress shop my friend told me about!" Mom suddenly cried. She led Madison over to a storefront decorated with lace, flowers, and little hearts. The sign out front read *Dress Up.*

"I don't know," Madison groaned, when she saw the frilly dresses and baby tees in the window. "This isn't really my style, Mom."

Mom put her hand on Madison's shoulder. "Let's go have a look before we jump to any conclusions."

Madison agreed to look inside, and they entered the store. She felt as though she'd been shoved headfirst into a bucket of potpourri. The whole place smelled like rose petals and cloves.

"Let's check out the clearance racks first," Mom said. She was always on the prowl for a good bargain.

The first dress Mom picked up was paler-than-pale blue with ruffles on top. It came down to the knee on Madison.

"This is like an old-lady dress, Mom," Madison said, putting the dress back on the rack. "I can't wear that. And it would be too hot, anyway. You're the one who said it's a thousand degrees in Texas."

Mom held out a second option in another shade of light blue. Madison frowned at the neckline. It had too many buttons.

"I'll sweat to death in this, Mom," she said.

"Well, how about this one?" Mom held out a yellow-and-white sundress.

"That's okay," Madison said with a shrug. "I could live with that." And so the yellow dress started an official try-on pile. Mom grabbed a couple of other dresses in Madison's size from other areas of the store, and they headed for the dressing room.

Madison squirmed in and out of sundresses, long dresses, tops and skirts and other wedding outfits for the better part of twenty minutes. Nothing fit quite right. If it wasn't too big, it was too snug or it was the wrong color or it was not "cool" enough for Madison's taste.

Just when she'd gotten almost completely dis-couraged, however, Mom handed Madison one more thing to try on.

Madison's eyes bugged out when she saw the simple, long dress her mom held out to her.

"Wow," she said to Mom. "I love this."

Mom grinned. "I knew you would. It was on that rack all the way across the store. I don't know how I missed it when we came in. It even has little sparkles sewn in and a ruffle on the bottom. . . ."

The dress was pale orange, almost a tie-dye design. Madison had never expected to find a formal dress that looked like that!

And it fit perfectly.

"I guess that look on your face means we'll get it," Mom said. "You're sure you like it? For a wedding? It is a little extreme. . . ."

"Mom! It's the best dress *ever*!" Madison said. "Stephanie will like it, too, I know it. She'll say it's so 'me.' We have to get it."

As they left the store and walked toward Central Shoes, a discount shoe store at the other side of the mall, Madison kept talking about just how "amazing" the orange dress was. When Mom stopped to check out a window display, Madison pulled the dress out to look at it again. While she was standing there, someone tapped her on the shoulder.

"You're Madison, right?" the girl asked tentatively. "Drew's friend?"

Madison turned and found herself face to face with Elaine Minami, Drew's neighbor from the pool party. Elaine's hair was pulled back with sparkly barrettes, and she wore faded jeans shorts and a tank top with little bees on it that read *Bee Nice* on the back.

"Oh . . . hi. Elaine, right?" Madison replied.

"I knew it was you!" Elaine chirped in her squeakiest voice ever. "What's up?"

"Um . . . shopping. I have this wedding. . . ." Madison mumbled.

"Really? Cool!" Elaine said. Madison considered herself to be a positive person, but Elaine put her to shame.

"Actually, my dad is getting married again," Madison admitted. "And I'm sort of in the wedding."

"Wow! That is cool!" Elaine said. "When is the wedding?"

"This weekend," Madison replied.

"No way! That is so soon!" Elaine said. She pointed to Madison's shopping bag. "Is that your dress?"

Madison opened the bag to show her the orange sherbet–colored dress, neatly wrapped in tissue paper from the store.

"Wow, that's different!" Elaine gushed. "I could never wear a dress like that. And it even sparkles. Cool."

"I like it," Madison said.

"What are you doing at the wedding?" Elaine asked. "Flower girl?"

"Junior maid of honor," Madison said.

"Really?" Elaine cried. "What a coincidence. I was a junior maid of honor, too. Just last fall, my aunt asked me to be one at her wedding. She made a big deal about the fact that it was way more important than just being a flower girl."

Madison was happy to hear that the title of junior maid of honor was a real thing and not just something Stephanie had invented to be nice. A surge of excitement sent tingles all the way down to her toes. For the first time all week, the wedding actually seemed . . . promising. Maybe her role in the ceremony *was* important?

"I'm also doing a reading," Madison added. "A poem."

Elaine's jaw dropped. "Get out! A reading! I didn't get to do anything as special as that. I just stood around holding flowers."

Madison smiled, feeling a strange sense of pride in her future wedding responsibilities.

"Well, my dad and his fiancée asked me to read this love sonnet by Shakespeare," Madison explained.

"That is soooo romantic!" Elaine said. "I hope that someone reads something that romantic at my wedding."

"*Your* wedding?" Madison giggled."You mean *after* junior high, right?"

"Yeah, of course!" Elaine giggled back. "I'm such a sucker for romantic stuff."

Madison's mom reappeared from the bookstore carrying a package.

"Hiya! Are you Madison's mom?" Elaine asked.

Mom smiled. "That's me. Are you a friend from school?"

Elaine shook her head. "No, I don't go to Far Hills. Madison and I met at Drew Maxwell's party yesterday."

"Yeah, Mom," Madison continued. "Drew and Elaine are neighbors in Far Hills Heights."

"I see. Do you want to join us for lunch, Elaine?" Mom asked.

"That would be great—but I can't," Elaine replied. "I'm actually on my way to meet Drew at the library in about fifteen minutes."

Madison knew that sometimes kids went to the library not to check books out, but to check *each other* out. She knew some kids who even kissed among the stacks. Was that what Elaine and Drew would be doing?

"Thanks for the invitation, though," Elaine said, hoisting her bag up over her shoulder. "See you soon, I hope!"

"See you!" Madison called out after Elaine.

Her insides squirmed as she watched Elaine weave through the crowd and onto an escalator.

Elaine and Drew sitting in a tree . . .

"She's a friendly girl," Mom commented.

"I think she and Drew are a couple," Madison said.

"Drew is dating?" Mom gasped. "Wait. Didn't you tell me that he had a crush on *you* at some point?"

"I guess his crush is over," Madison said dejectedly.

Mom gave Madison a hug and kissed the top of her head. "Sometimes I can't keep track of you kids," Mom said.

"How can people change their minds and feelings so easily?" Madison asked aloud.

"Do you mean Drew?" Mom asked as they continued walking.

"Maybe," Madison admitted. "But everyone else, too. How do you know if something is for real—that it will last?"

Mom shrugged. "There are no guarantees, ever."

"Mom, do you think Dad and Stephanie will last?" Madison asked.

Mom took her time answering the question. "That's hard to say," Mom admitted. "Nothing is ever a sure thing. But I do think that Stephanie and your father will be a nice match. He seems happy. So does she. That's all it takes."

"I wish you and Dad had lasted," Madison said, her true feelings slipping out even though she'd tried very hard to hold them in.

Mom kissed Madison once again. "Oh, honey bear," Mom said. "It's been a tough year."

Madison smiled. "Yeah," she said softly, giving Mom a small hug back. "I guess we should go find the wedding shoes now."

Working their way from one end of the mall to the other, Madison and her mom strolled past the *Roundabout*, the bloblike sculpture in the center of the mall. Madison lingered in front of the computer outlet store for just a second, and then they stopped off at the Ice Creamery. It was way too hard to resist the double chocolate chunk fudge ripple with marshmallows, so they shared some before lunch.

When they finally reached the shoe outlet, Madison was shocked to find the perfect pair right inside the window: a pair of orange Mary Janes—in just her size. Mom was worried that Madison might look a little too much like a Creamsicle, but Madison didn't care.

"It's my favorite color, Mom!" Madison cried. "And they match perfectly. I have to get them!"

After shoe shopping, Madison and Mom made their way back to the garage. Madison stopped short in front of a new store she spotted along the way. In the window was a huge display of stamps, paper, and various scrapbook materials. While Mom waited on a bench and made a call on her cell phone, Madison ducked inside to purchase a flower stamp, green foil for "leaves," and some ribbon for her wedding collage. The woman in the store even gave her some pointers on mixing different items together. Although the poem part wasn't coming along very well, Madison was getting super excited about all the other parts of her project. She bought some glitter glue, too.

When they arrived back home, Phinnie greeted Mom and Madison with a loud "Haruffffff!" and scratched at the door furiously until they came inside.

"Phinnie!" Madison said, dumping her bags on the couch and bending down to give him a squeeze.

"Let me remove the tags and other things from the dress," Mom suggested. "You really have to start thinking about what else you're going to pack, you know."

Madison nodded. "I know, I know." She was avoiding the inevitable.

While Mom dealt with the bags, Madison and Phin took the steps two at a time up to Madison's bedroom. Madison wanted to give her closet a once-over. Maybe some packing inspiration would strike—and maybe not.

The moment she stepped inside her bedroom, however, Madison's laptop tempted her, as if it had had the power to speak.

Madison, turn on my power button NOW!

Madison, of course, obeyed.

She powered the machine up and waited to see if she had any new e-mail. Lately, her e-mailbox had been emptier than usual, which was strange for summer. Usually everyone used e-mail (rather than the telephone) as the main way to keep in touch. Even stranger lately was the absence of e-mail from Bigwheels. Madison's keypal hardly ever delayed in writing back.

Madison scanned the list of names.

Her mailbox was not empty anymore!

FROM	SUBJECT
✉ Bigwheels	MY E-mail was down
✉ Boop-Dee-Doop	Ready 4 Summer Sale-o-rama
✉ JeffFinn	The Wedding (what else)

Madison clicked on the e-mail from Bigwheels first.

From: Bigwheels
To: MadFinn
Subject: MY E-mail was down
Date: Mon 15 July 11:21 AM

I feel like I've been sent to e-mail no-man's land. Last week I couldn't write b/c I had to babysit. Then our computer crashed. It was awful. My dad lost all these documents. He told me he wouldn't let me use it anymore, like he blamed me. I was worried I wouldn't be able to write to you ever again. Or at least not in time before u go to the wedding. Dad figured out what happened though and now he's even talking about getting me my own laptop just like u have. How cool is that?

SO that's why I didn't write over the weekend. What's new? Thanks for sending me e-mail about the pool party. U have cool friends in Far Hills. No one here has torches and smoothies at their parties. I'm jealous!

I have been collecting some ideas for you for the wedding collage ur making. I think u should write a poem about love but not just people love. Say you love ice cream and then shopping and books and the computer and all that and then u write about how loving ur Dad is all that plus more. Does that make any sense? I will think about it more.

Right now we're having neighbors over for this picnic dinner in our backyard. My mother likes to BBQ in the summer. At least the neighbors have a son (Tommy) who is kind of cute. He has like a billion freckles. I would flirt with him except I'm having majorly bad hair day frizz! LOL.

Wish you were here!
Yours till the cook outs,

Bigwheels aka Vicki

Madison hit REPLY to thank Bigwheels for her poem suggestions. She didn't say much more than that, though; and she certainly didn't share any of her poem attempts thus far. Bigwheels was very good at writing poems, and Madison couldn't even get two lines to work.

The next e-mail, from Boop-Dee-Doop, was an announcement of some great sale items like baby tank tops and chunky flip-flops, so Madison printed out the coupon code for the discount. She'd look over the Web site later with Mom and pick out a few things for the rest of the summer.

Last in the e-mailbox was a note from Dad. Getting e-mail from him was no big surprise. He'd been writing more than ever these days.

But what he had to say *was* surprising.

From: JeffFinn
To: MadFinn
Subject: The Wedding (what else)
Date: Mon 15 July 1:09 PM
News flash! I know you won't believe this, Maddie, but the wedding keeps on growing. Stephanie called home this morning and her mother now has a guest list of more than 150 people who are promising to show up! I realize when we first talked this was supposed to be a

small wedding but it's gotten a little bigger than that. I don't think I even know 150 people. Isn't this crazy? I called Rick and told him he needs to bring reinforcements. Ha-ha.

The reason I'm writing to tell you about it is so you can pack a few more "dressy" outfits. That's what Stephanie asked me to tell you. I guess there may be a few more dinners or events than I expected. I don't think it will be that formal, but you may want to have your mother help you choose some other dresses.

I'm at the office today and in meetings until seven but I will try to call later.

Love,

Dad

Madison bit her lip.

More *formal*? What did Dad mean by that? She tried to imagine 150 people in her living room, and it made her dizzy. Would she have to meet all those people? Or would Madison Francesca Finn get shoved into a corner somewhere with a mob of strangers while Dad and Stephanie rode off into the sunset? Even worse, how could she get up and read some sappy love poem in front of all those people? How could she smile and pretend to be happy the entire weekend? How was she going to find anything else to wear when it had taken her all afternoon to find just one dress?

Madison printed out her list of things to pack and then turned off her laptop. She grabbed a pen and threw herself onto the bed.

Trip To Texas: My Packing List So Far

Pale blue (not dark!) and yellow tank tops

Yellow T-shirt ➡ *check in laundry hamper!* ♥

Have a Heart T-shirt ➡ *check in laundry hamper!*

4 prs. underwear & my nice bra *(that doesn't show when I wear tanks or my new dress—don't forget!!)*

~~Jeans shorts (with fringes on edge)~~ ➡ *too casual?*

Jeans shorts with flower patch on side

Red capri pants ➡ *check in laundry hamper!* ❀

White skirt w/flowers

Kakki pants (is that how u spell it?) ✿

~~Pink sweater top~~ ➡ *too HOT??* ☀

White peasant blouse ➡ *borrow from Aimee ASAP*

New orange dress (for wedding)

Ask Fiona if I can borrow her purple sundress???

PJs (old T-shirt, Lisa Simpson shirt,)

Lip gloss (strawberry-kiwi and bubble gum)

Sneakers, black SANDALs, flip-flops, and new shoes (for wedding day)

Moonstone earrings (from Dad) and hangy bead earrings

Remind Dad to bring digital camera !!!

Laptop ➡ *w/everyone's email address*

****All stuff for making the collage—incl. tape and glue.

What else???????

Chapter 6

After she came inside from walking Phinnie very early on Tuesday morning, Madison went online. She had a lot of e-mail messages.

From: JeffFinn
To: MadFinn
Subject: More
Date: Tues 16 July 5:13 AM
Playing catch-up on some work this morning. There is so much to do before we leave for Texas. Wanted to send you all the information about the plane reservations, etc., for the wedding. I know your mother has probably been asking you. She mentioned something to me on the

phone. And don't forget there's a 2 hr. time difference. Texas is 2 hrs. behind us.

Sky High Airlines Flight 345
New York to Houston
Non-Stop Flight/Light Lunch
7/18 Departs New York, NY at 9:45 AM
7/18 Arrives Houston, TX at 12:15 PM

Sky High Airlines Flight 114
Houston to New York
Non-Stop Flight/Snack Only
7/21 Departs Houston, TX at 1:30 PM
7/21 Arrives New York, NY at 7:40 PM

I'm also attaching (below) an e-mail Steph sent to me about the extra stuff to pack. See if you can make sense of it. I'm so excited that I'm going to see you!

—Original Message—
From: Stephie8
To: JeffFinn
Subject: Madison Clothes
Date: Mon 15 July 11:13 PM

My mother says Madison needs to bring at least 3 nice outfits for each of the parties. She may want to pack more depending on the

weather. In addition to a nice
dress for the wedding itself I
think she should have another for
the rehearsal dinner, don't you?
Tell her that my nieces tend to get
all dolled up and I just want her
to feel comfortable. One of the
events will be a girls-only tea
party.

Talk soon.

Madison didn't even know what to think when
she read—and then reread—Stephanie's attachment.
She'd already freaked out enough the night before
about Dad's request to dress dressier. Now Madison
had to worry about some girls-only party?
Gulp.
The Wolfe girls would probably have perfect hair
and teeth and clothes and *everything*. Standing next
to them would be like standing next to Poison Ivy in
a lineup. Although Madison's enemy was evil, she
was always dressed just right. Madison couldn't even
get her hair to part the right way, sometimes. And
how was Madison supposed to look perfect in Texas,
a million miles from everything she knew and loved?
Double gulp.
Rather than think about it, Madison skipped on
to the next e-mail.
She was relieved to see that it was from her

favorite (and only surviving) grandmother, Mom's mom, Gramma Helen. Gramma Helen liked to check in on Madison now and again, usually to tell her some funny story or share a recipe. Madison wasn't a big cook, but ever since she'd baked Gramma's special muffins for a FHJH bake sale, Gramma had been forwarding all kinds of new and old recipes along. Today, however, she'd only sent a few words and no food ideas.

From: GoGramma
To: MadFinn
Subject: Keep Your Chin Up
Date: Tues 16 July 6:44 AM

I thought my hearing aid was on the fritz when your mother told me about your dad's wedding plans. I know it is hard enough to deal with parents splitting up only to watch them get married again to other people. I can only imagine what that feels like, my dear. If your grandfather were alive, he would say the same thing. Remember that we love you beyond all the things that change. So do your mom and daddy. I do think your dad is a good man. I wish him all the best. Tell him that I said that, would you? And for goodness' sakes, write your Gramma a note. It's been more than

two weeks, Maddie! I miss you
terribly when we fall out of touch.
Your mom said something about your
coming out to visit soon or maybe I
will go to NY. I hope I can do
that. Depends on the hip, as usual.

Keep your chin up high. And keep
your cool. No drooping allowed--not
even when it gets hot.

Speaking of which, how hot is it
there?

Love you,

Gramma

Madison sighed. Already she was exhausted from
thinking about the wedding festivities, and they had-
n't even begun. It was nice that Gramma Helen had
sent her good wishes to Madison's dad,
however. Madison would be sure to tell him about
that. Gramma hadn't seen Dad for a long time—since
way before the divorce. She would probably never
see him again—except maybe at *Madison's* wedding.
    And that was a century away.
    Madison felt a pang of nostalgia. She powered
down her laptop and headed for Mom's bedroom. Mom was busy selecting an outfit for a

special luncheon meeting later on that afternoon.

"You're having trouble picking out clothes, too?" Madison said. She fell onto Mom's unmade bed. Phin jumped up onto the bed beside her.

"Do you like the blue suit or the gray?" Mom asked.

Madison pointed to the blue. "That one. But I like your yellow dress better."

Mom smiled. "Me, too. But this is a serious lunch meeting with investors, and I need to look more serious than sunny."

"Mom, I don't have any clothes to pack," Madison cried.

Mom looked at her daughter severely. "Excuse me? We just bought you that new dress. You ordered some things online last month, too."

"Correction," Madison said, clearing her throat. "I don't have any clothes for Texas."

"Oh," Mom said. "Well, just throw some shorts and tops in a bag. You only have one big event, honey bear. And you have the perfect wedding outfit. Nothing to worry about."

"Correction," Madison said a second time. "Apparently, Mom, there are, like, ten parties in Texas, and Stephanie wants me to bring nice clothes for *all of them*."

"Are you kidding?" Mom said, looking as distressed as Madison had when she'd first learned about all the upcoming festivities.

"Yeah, I got an e-mail from Dad and Stephanie this morning," Madison said.

"Well, you must have something to wear," Mom said. "Look again."

"I do," Madison said. "But it's all old stuff. Can't we go shopping again and get another dress and maybe a skirt?"

Mom shook her head. "Maddie, we spent a lot of money on that new dress. I can't just go buying out the store every time there's another party. Why don't you look through your closet again and try to be creative? You're good at that."

"Will you help me?" Madison pleaded. "Please?"

Mom tossed the blue and gray suits back onto the bed and threw her hands up into the air. "Okay! But we need to make it fast—I have to get dressed. . . ."

They marched into Madison's room with Phinnie tailing them.

Mom pointed to a flowered sundress hanging at the side of the closet. "What about that?" she asked.

"But I got that in sixth grade," Madison said.

"And?" Mom replied. "You've worn it maybe twice."

"It doesn't fit," Madison stammered. She didn't want to bring the dress, no matter what. It looked very sixth-grade and not at all right for someone in junior high school.

"Fine!" Mom said, tossing it aside. "I'll start a

Goodwill pile then. What we don't wear, we won't keep. Moving right along . . ."

For almost an hour, Madison and Mom shuffled through Madison's closet at breakneck pace. By the time they were done, they'd successfully created two piles: one for giveaways and one for taking to Texas.

"I forgot I had this," Madison said, holding up a pretty blue dress with a sleeveless, lavender top. "I would have worn this a million times by now."

Mom rolled her eyes. "What a mess," she said.

Madison frowned. "Mom! I am not that messy. You should see Aimee's closet!"

"Mmm," Mom said. "I can't believe that you have three of the same pink T-shirt."

"Mom, it's no biggie. I just forgot I had them, that's all," Madison said.

"Have you even worn one of them?" Mom asked sharply. She was joking around, but her voice sounded serious.

Madison wanted to change the subject.

"Well, at least now I have whatever I need to bring. Except for the stuff that Aimee and Fiona are lending me," Madison said.

"Yes," Mom said. She pointed to Madison's suitcase. "That's true. Case closed."

Madison zipped her suitcase for the time being and then helped Mom lug two overstuffed shopping bags full of clothes downstairs. They would deliver them to Goodwill the following day. Mom's eye caught the digital readout on the kitchen stove.

"Oh, it's nearly ten-thirty!" Mom wailed. She had just an hour left to get ready for her big meeting. "Honey bear, I hate to pack and run, but I have to get ready," Mom said. "Are you sure you'll be okay here this afternoon without me?"

Madison nodded. "No sweat. I'll walk and feed Phinnie, finish packing, work on my wedding collage, and maybe I'll hook up with Aim or Fiona. I don't know. Maybe I'll clean my closet again?"

"Very funny," Mom said with a wink. "Just remember that you can call me on my cell phone if you need anything."

Mom was strict about insisting that Madison always stay in touch.

"Today will be great," Madison said, tossing a toy at Phin and settling onto the carpet for a game of doggy tug-of-war. "Quit worrying, Mom."

"But that's my job, dear," Mom said with a smile. She hurried back upstairs to get dressed.

As it turned out, Madison had more than enough to do at home to occupy the whole afternoon. She spent the late morning zipping and unzipping and repacking her suitcase, neatly folding and squeezing as much as possible into its small space. Madison made a mental note: *Ask for a bigger suitcase on my next birthday.*

After walking Phinnie (twice) and eating cold

pizza for lunch, Madison tried calling Fiona on the phone to see what she was doing. The line was busy. Aimee's phone line was also busy, so Madison went online. Maybe she could catch them in a chat room?

Aimee's name didn't show up on Madison's buddy list, but Fiona was online. Madison Insta-Messaged her right away.

```
<MadFinn>: were u on the phone?
<Wetwinz>: nooooo it was chet
   <GRRRRRRR>
<MadFinn>: what a drag I dunno
   what id do if I had 2 share my
   computer time
<Wetwinz>: maddie, SSS but I can't
   talk 4 long dad wants me to help
   him go pick up some stuff @ the
   store
<MadFinn>: r u guys still painting
   the basement
<Wetwinz>: yeah actually we're doing
   this cool mural
<MadFinn>: wow I can't wait 2
   see it
<Wetwinz>: BION Chet even painted
   some
<MadFinn>: did Egg come over?
<Wetwinz>: very funny
<MadFinn>: u spend so much time
   w/ur dad l8ly
```

<Wetwinz>: I always do in summertime
    esp. if I'm not in camp
<MadFinn>: do u think I'll see less
    of my dad after his wedding?
<Wetwinz>: OCN
<MadFinn> yah but do you think
    he'll stop telling me lame-o
    jokes all the time?
<Wetwinz>: OCN
<MadFinn> yah but
<Wetwinz>: oh maddie I have 2 go
    dad is here
<MadFinn>: I'll c u @ the cyber caf
    tomorrow right??
<Wetwinz>: totally
<MadFinn>: um, can i borrow
    something?
<Wetwinz>: sure what?
<MadFinn>: that purple sundress
    with the stripes along the bottom
    so I can wear it @ the wedding
    hoedown?
<Wetwinz>: no prob I'll bring it
    tomorrow
<MadFinn>: I promise I will take
    good care of it
<Wetwinz>: u can have my whole
    closet Maddie
<MadFinn>: :-{}
<Wetwinz>: KIR
<MadFinn>: bye!

Mom still wasn't home by the time Madison ended her chat with Fiona, so she opened a new file and started to write.

 Dad

What WILL life be like after Dad gets hitched?

I told Fiona I'd miss his bad jokes if he weren't around. But the truth is that I'd miss him way more than that. I'd miss his steak and fries and all the meals he makes for me. I'd miss his hugs. I'd miss his scratchy beard when he doesn't shave and his funny clothes.

Am I overreacting or will this marriage mean Dad goes on some kind of permanent vacation with Stephanie--and leaves me in the dust?

Rude Awakening: All my bags are packed. But I'm so NOT ready to go.

Chapter 7

Madison's eyes scanned the bookshelves at the Cyber Café. She wasn't sure she liked what she read.

Vow Power: Planning Your Second Wedding
Second Marriage, Fat Chance
Bring the Whole Family: The Brady Bunch
  Syndrome
Step-Parenting: Harder Than It Looks
Marry Me, Marry My Kids

"Do people really read this stuff?" Madison asked Aimee.

Aimee glanced over from where she was shelving some new books in the opposite aisle.

"I guess so," Aimee mumbled.

Madison and all her friends had come to the café for the afternoon because it was raining outside. It was no beach day.

The store was packed with customers. There were so many people shopping inside that Aimee's dad, Mr. Gillespie, had to crank up the air conditioner. The combination of rain and crowds of people had made it very humid in the store.

"Look what I found," Fiona announced, rushing around the corner with a stack of magazines. "Your dad said we could just have these."

Madison glanced over and saw a pile of old issues of *Star Beat*.

"But those are out of date now," Madison said.

"Yeah, but we can still tear out good hairstyles and clothes, right? Maybe there are some other ideas for what you can bring to the wedding," Fiona suggested.

"Hey, Maddie," Aimee said, pointing to a revolving rack. "Don't forget to check out postcards. My dad just got new ones. I bet you could use some for your wedding collage."

Madison's eyes lit up. "Cool," she said.

"AIMEE!" Mr. Gillespie called out.

Aimee made a face. When Aimee was at the bookstore, she couldn't just hang out. Mr. Gillespie always put her to work. "See you guys in a little bit," she said, heading around the corner to help her dad at the register.

Madison turned back to the books on marriage and romance.

"Hey, do you think you'll ever get married, Fiona?" Madison asked absentmindedly.

Fiona gasped. "Married? Maddie!" she cried. "That's too far into the future."

"Yeah, but if you had to make a guess . . ." Madison asked again.

Fiona smiled. "Sure," she admitted. "I guess I'll get married."

"Where?" Madison asked.

"Back in California," Fiona said wistfully. She still missed her old town and friends there. "That much I know for sure. On the beach. In my bare feet."

"That's so romantic—like in a movie," Madison said.

"And I would do it at sunset. It would have to be perfect. . . ." Fiona continued.

"Can you imagine what it must feel like to have someone ask?" Madison wondered aloud. "'Will you marry me?' It gives me chills."

"Maybe Egg will ask me to marry him someday," Fiona said, half jokingly.

"Oh, Fiona!" Madison wrinkled her nose. "That is just too weird to even think about. Egg?!"

"What about you, Maddie? Do you think you'll get married?" Fiona asked.

"Sometimes," Madison said with a shrug. "But then sometimes I wonder if I will ever even fall in love. . . ."

"Wait. You can't stress out about that yet. We're only in junior high," Fiona said.

"Yeah, but everyone always gets paired off," Madison said. "Except me."

Fiona leaned in for a hug. "That is *so* not true. My brother will never pair off with anyone," she cracked.

Madison laughed. "Oh, like that's supposed to make me feel better?"

"You know what I mean," Fiona said, still chuckling.

"I just wish I could meet someone I like who likes me right back. . . ." Madison said. As she spoke, their troop of guy friends appeared from around the corner. Chet and Egg led the pack. Hart was there, too, next to Dan.

Madison choked back her words.

How much had they heard?

Of course, deep, deep down, Madison dreamed that Hart would be the kind of guy she would marry. But she was too afraid to admit that out loud to anyone else except Phinnie and her long-distance keypal, Bigwheels.

"Hey!" Egg said.

"What are you doing?" Chet asked.

"Girl stuff," Fiona said. She did not take her eyes off Egg.

"You guys are *always* doing girl stuff," Chet groaned. He poked at a row of books next to his head.

Egg crouched down on the floor near Fiona. "We

87

were thinking of getting ice cream soon. Want to go?" he asked.

Madison watched Fiona bat her eyelashes at Egg as if she were a character in a cartoon.

"Okay," Fiona said softly.

Dan and Chet laughed at a joke book they were looking at.

Hart sidled up to Madison. "Looking for something?" he asked her.

She quickly glanced down at the bright-pink book in her hands.

Head over Heels: 101 Ways to Make Him Fall in Love with You.

Madison shoved the book under her armpit before Hart could read the title.

"No, nothing special . . . no, not really," Madison said, tongue-tied and losing her balance. She leaned sideways into the bookshelf.

Hart reached out and grabbed Madison's arm to pull her back.

"Oh!" Madison let out a little cry of surprise.

"Don't fall," Hart said, smiling.

All Madison could think was that she shouldn't fall in love with Hart. She regained her balance and still managed to hide the pink book from him.

"Actually, I was looking for a book for my mom," Madison lied.

"Really?" Hart said, a little distracted.

Madison realized that he didn't really care what

book she was holding or what book she was looking for. He was just being nice.

"So where's Drew today?" Madison asked him.

"Hanging with Elaine," Hart said with a grin. "He's helping set up a computer at her house."

"Oh," Madison said. She stared down at the floor.

"I think my cousin likes her," Hart admitted.

Madison lifted her head and tried to force a smile. "That's good for him," she said. "Elaine is nice, isn't she?"

"Elaine is like the nicest girl ever—" Hart started to say. "Except for you . . . and Fiona . . . and Aimee. Of course."

Madison faked a laugh. "Whatever," she said.

Hart laughed, too, and ran his fingers through his hair. "Yeah, whatever," he said, awkwardly.

What was with these guys? Madison wondered.

Aimee reappeared, pirouetting.

"Guess what?" Aimee said. "Dad says he'll treat us all to smoothies in the café if you guys want. That way we don't have to go outside to Freeze Palace and get wet."

By now, all the friends had gathered together in a huddle at the back of the store, and it reminded Madison of sitting at the orange table in the back of the lunchroom at FHJH.

"I want to check out the cyber stations first," Egg said. "We put our name on the waiting list. Can we get the smoothies after that?"

"Sure," Aimee said. "Whenever you want. The key thing is that they're FREE."

"Totally free!" Chet said. "Thanks, Mr. G."

Egg laughed out loud. "Gee, Chet, you're a poet and you don't even know it. Ha-ha-ha."

"Huh?" Chet said. "What are you talking about?"

Fiona rolled her eyes. "Dork," she said under her breath.

The other boys snickered and shuffled off to the computer area of the store.

"See you later, Finnster," Hart said.

Madison smiled. "Later," she said quietly. She watched him walk away.

"Maddie," Aimee whispered. "What's going on with you and Hart?"

Madison's eyes bugged out. "What are you talking about?"

"You were *so* flirting with him just now," Aimee said.

"I saw it, too," Fiona added.

Madison bit her lip. She felt her cheeks growing hotter than hot. "I was not flirting," Madison said defensively.

Aimee lifted an eyebrow. "You are the world's worst liar, Maddie," she said. "What's going on?"

"Yeah, I thought you liked Drew," Fiona said.

"What?" Madison cried. "You guys are making this stuff up. This is *so* not funny."

Aimee and Fiona giggled.

"Oh, Maddie, chill out," Aimee said.

"You chill out," Madison said.

Fiona poked Madison in the arm. "No, *you* chill out!"

"You guys! Quit it!" Madison said, throwing her arms into the air. "I'm going over to the computer stations. . . ."

"To see someone special?" Aimee teased.

"*Cut it out!*" Madison cried.

Someone in the next row over hissed, "Shhhhh!"

"We better shut up," Aimee said quickly. "Before Dad hears. He's always saying how noisy I am. . . ."

Madison made a face and walked away without looking back, not even when she heard her BFFs giggling behind her. She passed by a table of cat and dog calendars and "New Fiction" on her way into the café part of the store.

No sooner had she entered the "cyber" part of the store than she heard a voice yelling in her direction.

"Yo, Finnster!"

Madison gulped. Her girlfriends were *this* close to discovering the truth about Madison's crush, and she kept bumping into him in the store. This was way too close for comfort.

Madison looked over. "Hey, Hart," she said, without really looking into his eyes.

"Find any more books?" Hart asked, running

his fingers through his hair. He stood to the side of a computer terminal where Egg helmed the controls.

"Maddie!" Egg shouted, way too loudly. "You have to help me!"

Egg punched blindly at a bunch of keys. Hart just watched. Meanwhile, Dan and Chet sat at the next computer terminal checking out a NASCAR Web site.

"What's the address of the wedding page your dad did?" Egg asked.

"Why do you want *that*?" Madison sighed. She'd nearly forgotten about Dad's "We're Getting Hitched!" Web page. "Oh, Egg. You don't want to look at my dad's stupid page," Madison said.

"Yeah, I do," Egg replied. "Just tell me the address."

"His home page is his name," Madison said.

Egg typed it in. Up on the screen, Dad's work logo appeared. Below a scrolling list of pages for his company, Madison saw the links "Invitation," "Wedding Party," and "Sign Our Guestbook." In one corner was a small photo of Dad and Stephanie together. Egg clicked to enlarge it.

"Whoa, who's that?" Chet said, glancing over from his terminal.

"My future stepmother," Madison groaned as the now larger-than-life photo of Dad and Stephanie came into view.

"She's really pretty," Chet said.

"No kidding," Egg said, giving Madison a teasing little punch in the side.

She punched him right back—only harder.

"Ouch!" Egg cried.

"Your dad has a cool Web page," Hart said.

"He put a lot of new stuff up since you last showed it to me at the animal clinic," Dan said.

Madison cringed. Why were her friends looking at her dad's Web page? Why couldn't they flip back to NASCAR?

The boys clicked on "Sign Our Guestbook." A page with blanks to be filled in appeared. Egg typed in everybody's name. Then he asked the group, "What should I type for a message?"

"This is really dumb, Egg," Madison said. She wanted to melt into the floor.

"I know! Type in 'Congrats, Mr. Finn,'" Dan suggested.

Egg tapped out the words on the keyboard. He added: "From all of Maddie's friends."

"That looks cool," Chet said.

Everyone agreed. Egg hit SEND.

"What did you do that for?" Madison asked, sulking a little.

"I don't know," Egg said. "Because it was there."

The other guys laughed. Madison bent over and hit the OFF key on the computer.

"Hey!" Egg cried. "What did you do that for?"

"We're done here, right?" Hart said.

"Let's go get some of those free smoothies from Mr. Gillespie," Chet suggested.

"Yum," Dan said, eager to have something to eat. Sometimes friends referred to Dan as the "garbage disposal" at school. He would eat anyone's lunch leftovers, anytime.

"I'll go find Aimee and the others," Madison said, turning away from the boys. She wanted out of there—fast!

Luckily, the smoothies smoothed over any crabby moments, and the later afternoon delivered less embarrassment. At around three o'clock, the rain finally stopped. Egg convinced everyone to head down to Lake Dora to go swimming, even though the sky still looked cloudy.

"Oh, I can't go," Madison said.

Egg teased her. "Why not?" he complained. "You can't just ditch us. Come on. You're not mad about that Web page thing, are you?"

"No. I have to finish getting ready for Texas," Madison said. "Sorry."

"When are you leaving, again?" Dan asked.

"Tomorrow," Madison said.

"I can't believe you're going so far away," Fiona said, looking a little sad.

"Give me a break," Chet cracked to his twin sister. "You're such a drama queen. She's only going for a wedding."

"But the trip is five days," Aimee corrected him. "And that is a long time."

"It'll go fast," Egg said.

"I'll miss you," Fiona said, reaching out to embrace Madison.

"Me, too," Aimee said.

Madison hugged her friends right back. "Me, three," she said.

"Gag me," Chet moaned.

Egg patted Madison on the back. "See you around, Maddie," he said. "Say hi to your dad for me. For real."

"Yeah," Dan chimed in.

"Have a good trip, Finnster," Hart said with a wave of his hand.

"I will," Madison said, unable to take her eyes off Hart's tousled hair. For a split second, she had an overwhelming urge to throw her arms around him and give him a hug.

But she resisted.

Aimee handed Madison a blue-and-yellow envelope with little flowers along the edges.

"Take this for the plane ride," she said.

"What is it?" Madison asked.

Fiona beamed. "It's a surprise," she said. "From both of us. But you can't read it until you get on the plane. Promise?"

"Promise."

Madison glanced up at the wall clock over the

store register. Mom would be coming by the store in a few minutes to take her home.

"I'd better go," Madison said.

She raced out of the store and onto the slick streets outside. There, she stood by the glass doors of the Cyber Café waiting for Mom and fingering the blue-and-yellow envelope in her pocket.

She inhaled deeply, breathing in the smell of rain and grass; she craned her neck and gazed up at the lightening sky.

In one day, she would be in Texas, Madison thought.

Wow.

She reached out for the side of the building to keep from falling over. There was no Hart to grab her arm right now. Madison was on her own for the weekend—and for longer than that, she feared.

In three days, Dad would be married all over again.

If anything had ever felt as scary as the Big D, this was it.

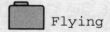 Flying

The last time I was on a plane was when I traveled with Mom on one of her business trips for Budge Films. She was making a movie and we went to this jungle. That was different. The bugs were HUGE. Right now I feel a little like I'm flying into another jungle. Why am I so nervous about this wedding?

Dad is sitting across from me right now and we're in this airport lounge/waiting room. Stephanie already flew to Texas a few days ago on her own so Dad keeps calling her on his cell. It is a little annoying b/c I wish he'd pay a little more attention to me, but I get it since it is his wedding and he's thinking about her 24/7. He let me buy all these magazines at the newsstand so I forgive him.

Not so good: I cheated BIG TIME and read Aimee and Fiona's plane letter before getting on the plane. Bad Maddie! But they don't have to know, right? I was dying to read it. The envelope was all crunched from being in my pocket. I have to write back to them now. Plus I have to write to Bigwheels too. I've been so busy that I have hardly checked my e-mail in the last day. I wonder if she wrote to me first? She probably thinks I dropped off the face of the Earth.

Someone just came on the speaker to announce the pre-boarding of our flight to Houston. We already checked our luggage. I squeezed as much as I could into my suitcase so all I have to carry on the plane with me is secret wedding collage stuff (in case I want to work on it), the magazines, and my laptop of course that fits in my orange bag.

I miss Mom and Phinnie already. Mom made me pancakes with smiley faces this morning. She still doesn't seem upset about Dad getting married. How is that possible? Didn't she love him a lot once? If I was married to someone for so long and then they married another person, I would be way upset. At least I think

I would be.

My head is all woozy right now.

Rude Awakening: I feel like I'm flying and we haven't even gotten on the plane yet.

Dad gently tapped Madison on the shoulder.

"That's us, honey," he said, grabbing his carry-on bags and garment case. "Ready?"

Madison wanted to scream, "Ready? What, are you kidding me? Of course I'm not ready, Dad! Duh! What are you *thinking*?"

But instead she stood up, too, grabbed her orange bag, and quietly followed Dad back into the main terminal, toward Gate B15. According to the flight supervisor, who spoke with a distinct Texas twang, Sky High Airlines had just commenced "general boarding for all passengers headed to the Lone Star State." Her voice crackled over the loud-speaker.

Madison and Dad took seats near the entrance to the gate, waiting for their seat numbers to be called.

"Dad?" Madison asked meekly.

"What is it, hon?" Dad said, struggling to balance his luggage in a neat pile on the floor next to him.

"Are you nervous?" Madison asked.

"About flying?" Dad replied. "Nah."

"No, no, that isn't what I mean," Madison said. "I mean, are you nervous about *getting married*?"

"'Course," he said matter-of-factly.

"Because I'm nervous about you getting married," Madison admitted.

Dad paused. "Everything will be fine, Maddie," he said, trying to reassure her.

"Tell that to all the butterflies in my stomach," Madison said.

Dad laughed. "I'm sorry that you're nervous," Dad said. "What can I do to make it better?"

Madison sighed. That was really all she needed—or wanted—to hear. She wanted to know for sure that Dad cared and hadn't forgotten her. She wanted to know that he would be there for her—especially if she was feeling crummy.

The boarding attendant called their seat numbers, and Madison followed Dad into the plane. It was only half full, so even though they technically had only two seats in a three-seat row, they were able to spread out. Madison sat next to the window. That way, she could turn slightly, blocking Dad's view of what she was up to. She could read her plane letter and work on the collage some more.

As soon as the plane took off, Madison uncrumpled the blue-and-yellow envelope from her BFFs.

Hello, Maddie!

This is an attempt to write you the best and hopefully the longest plane letter in the history of plane letters--EVER. You better be on the plane when reading this or else! Fiona and I are sooooo sad that you have to go away in the middle of the summer to someplace so far away but we know you will have a wicked good time. Okay it's Fiona's turn to write now.

Hello Maddie!!!!! Have you ever gotten a letter from two people at once? Isn't this cool? We miss you already, so you have to write to us like every single day when you are in Texas, okay? Sorry my writing is so small. Can you read it? I hope so. Where are you sitting on the plane? What did you wear? I bet you look awesome like you always do.

Wait I have a question 4 you: is Drew going out with that girl we met at the party? We promise to keep an eye on them while you are away because we know you secretly like him ha ha ha ha J/K

I didn't say that. That was totally Aimee's idea! I know u don't like Drew and it isn't fair to make fun of him either. Sometimes Aim can be such a meanie. LOL. Anyway, I haven't been on a plane in so long. It must be so cool to be flying. Just how long is the trip to Texas? What else did you pack? I know you will look good in my sundress. You have to write and tell us AS SOON AS YOU GET THERE and go to parties.

Okay, sorry sorry sorry about that Drew comment b4--I just think it is so weird that ANYONE would date him I guess. Meanwhile, did I tell you that Ben called me up? He did. I guess he wanted to ask me to a movie or something but he had to do something with his parents instead. Lame-o. I am so bummed out. I know I was embarrassed about liking him b4 but I'm not anymore. What do you think? You have to write and tell me, okay? I miss you already, Maddie. I wish the wedding wasn't so far away. BTW: Will there be dancing at the wedding? What dancing do they do at hoedowns?

Aimee asks the most random things, doncha think? OK since you are on a plane, we both made this list of other questions that you have to fill in about the trip--and then you can see if the answers come true after the weekend is over. Have you ever done that before? I did a going to camp letter once and put into it that I wanted to win a soccer medal and I wanted to meet a boy and I did BOTH. So I think this letter is kind of like a good luck charm. You have to write answers like what you HOPE will happen.

1. What will you see when you get off the plane?

2. Who will you meet at the party in Texas? (Like hot guys!!!)

3. What will you wear to the wedding (including how you will fix your hair)?

4. How many e-mails will you send to Aimee and Fiona? (And this answer must be at least five. One for every day you are away. OK?)

Wait a minute Maddie, are you going to see Stephanie's nephew at the party? What is his name again? Craig? Chris? I can't remember!!!! completely forgot to ask you about him. I know you were supposed to meet him a couple of times before. I wonder if he's cute. Have you ever seen a picture. You didn't say anything to us so we were wondering. I really wish I were going to the wedding too not just because it would be fun to go to Texas but so I could meet Craig and any other boys at a real wedding. Aren't people there all mushy all the time? I've never been to a wedding so I have no clue but I hope so for your sake. Oh I cannot wait to hear all about it!!!! ☺ ☺ ☺

The most important thing to remember Maddie is that WE LOVE YOU SO MUCH and WE MISS YOU SO MUCH and you shouldn't ever stress out because we are here for you 1000 percent. We will be right here the whole time you are gone. I hope that makes you feel better. Does it make you feel better? IT BETTER!!!!!

I know Fiona said this already but you have to write to us the very minute you get off the plane. You can E us from Texas right? We will try to get online & maybe we can have a chat on bigfishbowl.com or something too. I know Fiona will be home a lot while her Dad gets better (yeah) so we'll both write back a lot. And Blossom and I will keep an eye on Phinnie while U are gone. Maybe he can even sleep over our house one night as long as my brothers don't torture him HA HA J/K Bye for now! Love, Aim

P.S. Don't forget to send us a copy of the stuff you make on the wedding collage. If we get any ideas for you we'll send them. I know it will kick butt. LYLAS! xoxxooxoxxoxoxoxo Fiona

The flight was supposed to be four hours long, but it took five. Madison consumed three bags of minipretzels, two root beers (she couldn't believe they had her favorite drink on the plane!), and a rubbery turkey sandwich with a wilted salad. They showed a movie that she'd never seen, but the headset on her armrest didn't work. She moved into the center seat of the row to watch, while Dad snoozed. He said he hadn't had a good night's sleep in a week.

While Dad slept, Madison had another opportunity to work on her collage. She had already clipped out magazine pictures of happy faces and flowers. And she had glued a blue cord all around the edge of the page. Madison fiddled with more paper to finish it up. It was harder without scissors (which were absolutely not allowed on the plane for security reasons), but Madison discovered that she actually liked the torn edges even better than neat ones.

Best of all, Dad didn't wake up once.

Once the plane landed, Dad grew fidgety—and more than a little grumpy, which was unusual for him. Madison had never seen him like that before. What had happened to Dad, who usually cracked jokes in stressful situations?

It was also two hours earlier in Texas than it was in Far Hills. Madison reset her watch to match the clocks in the Houston airport.

Dad hurried them into the terminal. They followed the signs for the baggage-claim area. Madison couldn't wait to get the luggage and go. Stephanie would be meeting them on the lower level.

Standing at the top of the escalator looking down, Madison saw her future stepmother waving frantically.

"Hello, y'all!" Stephanie called out with a drawl Madison had never heard her use before. The old Texas had crept back into her voice.

Dad's face broke into a wide grin.

"Are you ever a sight for sore eyes!" Dad called out, giving Stephanie a warm hug. He turned back to Madison. "What a flight we had!"

Stephanie leaned over and planted a kiss on Madison's cheek. "You look stellar, as usual," she said. "Everyone's dying to meet you."

"Me, too," Madison said. And the truth was, now that they'd arrived in Texas, Madison did feel excited about being there, about being in a wedding, and about going to a real, live hoedown. She could feel the hot, Texas air coming through the doors every time someone walked in or out—and she liked it.

"Our bags are on the third carousel," Dad said, pointing. They walked over and waited about ten minutes before it even started to move. Madison stared as each bag was unloaded onto the conveyor belt. She watched suitcases go around . . . and around . . . and around. . . .

"There's my attaché case!" Dad cried. "And my other garment bag. Great!"

Madison kept watching for her suitcase, but she didn't see it.

Slowly, the other people on their flight retrieved their pieces of luggage, so that, one by one, the bags disappeared from the carousel.

Madison's bag still had not arrived. She got a lump in her throat.

"Dad!" Madison cried. "Where is it?"

Stephanie rubbed her back. "Let's go ask someone," she suggested, pointing to the customer-service window.

They walked over and, after speaking with an attendant, arranged to put a trace on the missing suitcase.

Madison dropped her head in her hands. "Oh, Dad. This is a nightmare," she said. "Everything is in that suitcase. *Everything*."

"You'll be okay, honey," Dad said. "We'll get it back. I promise."

More promises, Madison thought. More promises she knew Dad had no control over.

"Maddie, I wouldn't worry. I know it's a real drag now, but usually, they find the case right away," Stephanie said. "And the airline will have it delivered out to the ranch. No problemo."

Madison wasn't encouraged. "What about my clothes? What about my dress for the wedding? It took me all week to pack."

She wanted to cry.

"Let's see what happens," Stephanie said, trying to calm Madison. "We will call later—and we can always drive back tomorrow and check into it."

"We can?" Madison was happy to have any encouragement.

Stephanie reassured her. "This is some crazy weekend, huh?"

Madison chuckled softly. "Yeah," she agreed. "Hilarious."

They walked through a set of sliding doors and out into the Texas sun.

"Whooeee!" Stephanie exclaimed. "Hot enough for you?"

Dad wiped his brow. "I'll be changing out of these clothes as soon as we get to the hotel."

Madison's stomach did a flip-flop. *She* didn't have any clothes to change into. She wondered what else was in store for the rest of the wedding weekend.

The drive from the Houston airport to Stephanie's hometown of Bellville took an hour. Madison rode in the backseat as they cruised through the towns of Katy and Sealy. Madison gazed at the scenery as it rolled past. She was hermetically sealed inside the air-conditioned car, so she didn't feel the heat that went along with the scenery.

"You're in cowboy country now," Stephanie announced as they closed in on Bellville.

Madison didn't see any cowboys riding horses or

wearing big hats. At first, Bellville seemed like other towns Madison had visited, in other states: lots of trucks, strip malls, and houses scattered along the road.

Where were all the megaranches?

"We'll stop at the hotel first," Dad said to Madison.

They pulled up in front of the Bellville Villas. A parking attendant helped them their remove their bags from the car, and then the three of them headed inside to check in.

The hotel lobby was drenched in sunlight. It had an atrium roof and plants hanging everywhere. Mexican blankets, pillows, and tapestries covered big leather couches and chairs around the room. The air inside was warm, but giant ceiling fans kept the room cool. Madison gazed through the lobby to the sliding-glass doors in back that led out to a terra-cotta-tiled pool. It was like a hotel Madison had seen once on television.

Dad rented a room for Madison to stay in all by herself, adjoining his room. After claiming his reservation, he smilingly handed Madison the key card to her room, number 304.

"Here you go, big girl," Dad said.

Madison cringed. "Dad, do you have to call me that?"

Dad and Stephanie explained to the hotel receptionist about Madison's missing luggage. There were no "we found it" messages from the airport—yet.

The hotel promised, however, that, as soon as the bag came in, it would be sent up to the room immediately.

Madison sighed. She realized that she would have to stay in her sticky traveling clothes until the bag arrived. That meant having dinner that night in the same outfit she'd scrunched and wrinkled up throughout the flight to Texas. Her pants also had some weird stain on them, probably from the cranberry juice she'd drunk on the plane.

"Maddie, you look fine," Stephanie tried to reassure her.

Madison didn't believe her.

"Are we going up to the room for a little while?" Madison asked.

Stephanie nodded. "I know your dad wants to wash up, and we have a few phone calls to make. . . ."

Moments later, they were inside the elevator on the way up to the third floor. The hallways were decorated with pictures of cowboys and desert framed in gold leaf, and the red wallpaper felt like straw. The hall was dead quiet. Madison got to her room first and poked the key card into the door.

"Whoa!" she cried, rushing into the room and throwing her orange bag onto one of the double beds. She had a T.V. cabinet, a sofa, and even a minifridge!

"This is very nice," Dad said aloud, squeezing

Stephanie's hand as the two of them stood in the doorway of Madison's room. He pulled his fiancée closer. "No, this is *perfect*," he said, kissing her on the lips.

Madison looked away. "Um . . . I have to p—p—p—pee," she stuttered.

"Well, we're going next door to our room," Dad said. "Why don't you hang out for a little bit before we head over to the Wolfe ranch for supper? I'll come knock on the door in about an hour, okay?"

Madison nodded. "Okay, Dad," she said, ducking into the bathroom.

Through the bathroom door, she could hear Dad and Stephanie kiss one more time before they left Madison's room.

Alone at last! Madison said to herself, emerging from the bathroom as soon as her dad and Stephanie had gone. She surveyed her very own space, hardly able to believe that Dad had rented her a room of her own. But course he had! Dad was getting married that weekend. Bunking with him was out of the question. Duh. And Uncle Rick and Aunt Violet wouldn't be arriving for a day or two—and were only staying for one night, so she couldn't stay with them.

Madison had to admit that she really *did* feel like a big girl. She sat down on her bed and bounced a few times, clicking the remote control to see what was on Texas T.V. after four o'clock. Flicking past talk shows, game shows, and local news, Madison turned the tube back off again.

Why watch T.V. when she could e-mail Aimee and Fiona? Madison had promised to do it as soon as the plane landed. That was now.

It took a while to figure out how to dial up a local connection and go online to bigfishbowl.com, but Madison figured it out, and soon enough she was sitting inside the Web site chat room looking for her BFFs.

Aimee wasn't online. But Fiona was.

```
<MadFinn>: IMY!!!
<Wetwinz>: you rock for writing
    right away IMY2!!
<MadFinn>: Texas is hotter than hot
<Wetwinz>: I wanna talk 2 u I had a
    terrible day
<MadFinn>: oh no what is it
<Wetwinz>: Egg canceled on me
<MadFinn>: No way what happened
<Wetwinz>: he asked me 2 the movies
    and then he bailed
<MadFinn>: y?
<Wetwinz>: he said his Mom had some
    family dinner and he had to help
    out but I don't believe him
<MadFinn>: Oh Fiona :>(
<Wetwinz>: what if he wants 2 break
    up w/me
```

```
<MadFinn>: relax that's not going to
   happen
<Wetwinz>: meanwhile Chet knows Egg
   canceled and so he's been teasing
   me all day long--ANNOYING
<MadFinn>: what did ur parents say?
<Wetwinz>: they don't know and im
   not telling
<MadFinn>: I think u should blow it
   off and I bet Egg calls u tomorrow
<Wetwinz>: u think so?
<MadFinn>: Fiona it will be ok
<Wetwinz>: but I have a bad feeling
```

Madison told Fiona at least four more times that Egg would call to reschedule their date. She wished she could just skip over to Fiona's house to offer advice instead of having to help her BFF via e-mail. Long-distance wasn't the same.

Madison glanced up at the digital readout on the phone. It said 4:52. Dad would be knocking in ten minutes. She quickly signed off with Fiona and went in to her e-mailbox to type a long overdue note to Bigwheels.

```
From: MadFinn
To: Bigwheels
Subject: We're Heeeeere
Date: Thurs 18 July 4:54 PM
```
How r u? Time is going by fast. But
we got here in one piece.

Unfortunately the airline lost my luggage. Can u believe that? My whole life is in my dumb suitcase-- and I'm stuck in the same icky clothes until it arrives. You're as superstitious as me, right? So what kind of a bad sign is THIS? (:--

So far Texas is sweaty (at least I am) but it's pretty 2. I keep seeing the coolest wildflowers along the road, way dif from my mom's garden @ home. But I will probably draw a few of them onto my collage present so it looks like I included Texas.

This town we're in is called Bellville and Stephanie told me there are more than 170 cemeteries here. Is that a lot? Right across the street from the hotel there is also this old jail that's so cool looking like in a western movie or something. Dad says they have a real gallows like a place where people could be hanged but I guess only one guy ever died there back in 1901. Still creepy, huh? I wonder if the hotel is haunted? As if I wasn't worrying enough about this weekend, now I'm thinking about ghosts.

Tonite we're going to have a quiet (I hope) dinner with Stephanie's family on their ranch and then tomorrow is a free day. I think. Stephanie said something about it being a "girl" day but what does THAT mean?

Write back soon?

Yours till the cow pokes,

MadFinn

p.s. Can you imagine if my suitcase doesn't arrive in time and I have to wear these same exact clothes tomorrow AND the day after that? I wish there was a hotline 1-800-HELP ME NOW!!! If I have to be in these same shorts for more than tonight, I am locking myself in the hotel room. Wouldn't u? I better check the list of wedding activities to see what I'll be missing. LOL.

Welcome to Wolfe Ranch

Celebrating the Marriage of
Steph & Jeff
July 18 – 21

Thursday, July 18
Homecooked Grub at the Ranch
(family only)

Friday, July 19
Family Breakfast at Monica's Café
Girls-Only Wedding Tea Party
Boys-Only Fishing Trip
Rehearsal Ceremony at Bobcat Lake,
Wolfe Ranch
Dinner at the Great Hall
in Bellville City

Saturday, July 20
The Main Event, Wolfe Ranch
Wedding Ceremony
Hoedown Under the Stars

Sunday, July 21
Bon Voyage Breakfast BBQ at the Ranch

Bellville, Texas

It was almost five-thirty by the time Madison, Dad, and Stephanie got into the car and headed over for the "family-only" dinner at Wolfe Ranch.

Dad finally got a callback from Sky High Airlines at the Houston airport. The attendant there said that Madison's missing suitcase had been located. Unfortunately, it was somewhere in Wisconsin, but they were sure it would make a safe landing in Texas *eventually*. Madison tried not to think about her luggage falling out of a plane and landing on some poor cow in a field in the middle of nowhere or just lying around some deserted airport.

The drive to the Wolfe house meandered through downtown Bellville, past galleries and shops and at least five different saloons. Stephanie gave a guided tour, pointing to landmarks as they passed. Just outside town, Madison saw her first real cowboy, a man in a Stetson hat riding a beautiful, chestnut-colored horse. Stephanie waved to him. Apparently, he was an old friend.

"Who's that again?" Dad asked.

"My cousin Tony, remember? you met him once," Stephanie said. "He'll be at the wedding for sure!"

Dad wrinkled his eyebrows at her remark. Madison wondered just how many people were in the final wedding count by now, this close to the big event. Would Tony or any other cowboys be riding horses to the ceremony?

That would be cooler than cool.

They drove past more office buildings, several enormous gas stations and shopping marts, and some new housing developments. The homes were all of the same color and construction. There were some complexes with names like Vaqueros Village (Madison learned that *vaqueros* meant "cowboys" in Spanish). There were few trees.

"There's been a real boom around here," Stephanie said. "A lot of folks have discovered this area lately. Nothing like when I was a little girl. Used to be quiet around these parts."

"How far is your family ranch?" Madison asked from the backseat.

"About five miles. Pretty close," Stephanie replied.

"Wait until you see this place," Dad said, turning his head to see Madison. "It's like a dude ranch from some movie."

Madison felt the butterflies acting up in her tummy once more. Even though Dad was right there, close by her in the front seat, Madison felt alone. She wished Fiona or Aimee were there to crack jokes about meeting dudes at the dude ranch or horsing around with horses or something equally silly. Although she knew she was one hundred percent welcome there in Texas, Madison was having pangs of outsider angst that only got worse as the ranch began to come into view. She wished more of Dad's family would be attending—if only Dad had had more family *to* attend. Right now, Madison was becoming painfully aware again of the fact that she had few aunts, uncles, or cousins on her dad's side.

The gates of Wolfe Ranch had a large sign posted with the ranch's name on it in English and Spanish, alongside a pair of giant horseshoes. That was the ranch's theme, if there was one—horseshoes on every gate and post.

"My parents have always believed horseshoes are lucky charms," Stephanie explained.

Madison gazed at the rows and rows of trees that lined the driveway up to the main house. The tree branches looked like the craggy arms and legs of the trees that came alive in the forest in *The Wizard of Oz*. Madison felt her imagination working overtime.

After a short ride, they drove around a bend, and the main house came fully into view.

"Wow," Madison said, catching her breath. "It *is* huge."

Not only was the main house enormous, but Madison noticed about six other buildings nearby, a stable across the way, cars parked everywhere, numerous people rushing all around, and at least seven dogs running around free.

"I wish Phinnie were here," Madison mused.

"Yeah," Stephanie said. "He'd love roaming around here. My parents' dogs would show him a real good time."

After parking the car, Stephanie threw her arms around an older man who came to help carry the bags. Madison guessed correctly that the man was Stephanie's father, Wally.

"Are you Maddie?" the man asked, extending his arms for a hug from Madison.

Madison nodded and gave him a hug. His soft beard smelled like cedar and cigars.

"Hello," Madison said. "Nice to meet you."

"Looks like you've got a lot of guests here, Wally," Dad said, shaking his hand.

"Indeed. The troops have arrived," Mr. Wolfe replied. "Steph, your mother has gone all out for this one, let me tell you. Bigger than any of your sisters' weddings, and she pulled it off in only two weeks. Astounding woman, that one."

Stephanie laughed, but Madison noticed that Dad didn't seem to find it as funny. His eyes searched the property, taking in the scene of organized chaos.

"The family is in the courtyard," Mr. Wolfe said. "Shall we go see 'em?"

Madison followed Stephanie, Mr. Wolfe, and Dad inside through a set of nicely carved wooden doors. She expected to find maybe five or even ten people mingling around a table set with corn chips and salsa (a Texas-style snack). Instead, Madison saw at least forty people crammed together drinking frozen fruit drinks and talking at the tops of their lungs. When Stephanie appeared with Dad, the entire courtyard burst into a round of applause.

It was like being at one of Drew's pool parties— only bigger and even more extravagant.

"Here comes the bride!" a voice sang out.

A round, plump woman wearing sequins toddled over and grabbed Stephanie's waist.

Sequins?

Madison looked down at her shorts. She was definitely not dressed properly.

"Hello, Mother," Stephanie said. "They made it in one piece, just like you said."

"Welcome home!" Mrs. Wolfe said. "Jeff, I have to tell you that when we learned the plane was late, Steph almost fainted. I think she's a little nervous. What d'you think?"

"I think you look ravishing tonight," Dad said,

leaning over to give Mrs. Wolfe a big kiss. She let out a holler.

"And *you* must be Maddie! As pretty as your pictures," Mrs. Wolfe said, directing her attention to Madison.

All at once, Madison felt herself wanting to cling to Dad's leg as she probably had when she was two or three years old.

"Nice to meet you, Mrs. Wolfe," Madison said.

"Call me Diane, please!" Mrs. Wolfe barked.

Mrs. Wolfe grabbed Madison right around her middle and squeezed. Madison could feel the sequins sticking to the exposed areas of her skin. "You look good enough to eat!" she told Madison.

"Thanks," Madison said, imagining herself as dinner's main course, Tacos Madison with Not-So-Hot Sauce.

"Ma, why don't we sit down?" Stephanie suggested.

"Nonsense!" Mrs. Wolfe said. "You have *guests*!"

Madison saw Stephanie grab Dad's hand; they pulled themselves toward each other like magnets.

People started to flood over and bid their good wishes to Stephanie, Dad, and even Madison, who stood back and tried to take the scene in without being overwhelmed by it.

"I'd like you to meet cousin Jayne. . . . Uncle Wayne . . . Aunt Miranda . . . Uncle Fred . . . Cousin Billy-Carl . . ."

Madison's head whirled. There was no way she could remember all of those people. She smiled politely as each one was introduced.

"This is Steph's new daughter-to-be!" Mrs. Wolfe said, pointing to Madison. "She'll be doing the big reading at the wedding!"

Madison hated it when adults talked about her as if she weren't even in the room. It made her want to run away.

But she stayed put. Instead of making a mad dash, Madison popped a miniature-corn appetizer into her mouth and kept smiling.

Dinner was casual, just as the wedding itinerary had promised. Hot and cold items were displayed on wide, plank tables decorated with lanterns, maracas, and an ice sculpture in the shape of a giant cactus. Madison said "thank you" and "please" and worked her way around the food table. She noticed a few kids her age who came in looking for stuff to eat, and guessed that they'd all been hanging out somewhere else together.

One kid in particular caught Madison's eye.

Or, rather, she caught *his* eye.

The boy looked right at Madison from across the food table and said, "Hey!" as if he were a cowboy or something.

"Hey," Madison giggled. She couldn't help herself.

The boy grabbed a handful of tortilla chips and

walked away without saying another word. His friends (or were they all cousins?) left the room with him.

Madison bit into a sweet pickle and cursed her traveling shorts that by now had a little spot on one of the cuffs. She was sure that her outfit had been the key factor in driving the boy away. The room closed in on her, hotter by the minute, even though both the air-conditioning and the fans were going. People melted together in a weird combination of heat and noise and color.

Madison sat down in a leather chair and sipped a cup of cream soda. It wasn't as good as root beer, but it would have to do.

"Maddie?" Dad said, bending down to check on her. "Are you okay?"

Madison nodded as if to say, "Sure, I'm fine," but her words came out a different way.

"I don't know anyone, Dad," Madison said softly. "Who *are* all these people?"

Dad smiled and crouched down closer to Madison. "They're Stephanie's family," he explained. "And I know it's overwhelming. It was—it *is*—for me, too. They seem to travel in packs, like . . ."

"Wolfes," Madison said, cracking the bad joke before Dad could.

Dad smiled. "Exactly," he said. "Have you met any of Stephanie's nieces or nephews?"

Madison shook her head silently, without mentioning the boy who had caught her eye.

122

Stephanie rushed over. "Jeff! Come over here! You have to meet Ed, my dad's old business partner. He's like my second daddy, really."

"I was just sitting with Madison for a minute," Dad said.

Stephanie pasted on a pout. "Aw, sweetie, come for just a minute, won't you? He's dying to meet you. Maddie will be okay on her own for a minute, won't you?"

Madison sank into the chair a little. She could feel Dad pulling away.

"Will you be okay, Maddie?" he asked.

Madison felt her palms sweating. The room was getting even hotter, if that were possible. Because she was sitting and everyone around her was standing, Madison felt as if she had been shrinking into the furniture.

"No, Steph," Dad said all of a sudden. "Maddie isn't feeling well. I'll meet Ed later. He'll understand."

Stephanie didn't say anything at first. Madison had never really known Dad to tell her no before that.

"Okay," Stephanie finally said. "We'll meet him later, then."

She rubbed her hands together, smiled, and turned back to the party with a flourish.

"I'm sorry, Dad," Madison said after Stephanie had walked away.

"No, I'm sorry," Dad said. He reached up and felt

123

Madison's forehead. "You're warm, honey bear," he said. "Maybe you can go and lie down?"

Madison shrugged. She didn't want to lie down in some strange room. She remembered having done that a couple of years back at a party with Mom and Dad. She had ended up asleep on someone's guest bed. She had awakened in the dark to find herself alone with a pile of woolen coats.

"I'll be fine," Madison said.

Dad cocked his head. "Are you *sure*?" he asked again.

Madison took a deep breath. "I just didn't expect such a big wedding party," she said. "And my suitcase got lost. . . . and we're so far from Far Hills. . . ."

"I understand," Dad said.

"Dad, I thought you said—you *promised*—this would be fun. You said it wouldn't be that many people. If there are this many people here tonight, what's tomorrow's dinner going to be like?" Madison asked.

"I know," Dad said. "It's a lot."

Madison felt her eyes well up with tears. "It is," she said, her voice quivering a little bit.

Dad gave her a hug. "It is for me, too," he said.

"Really?" Madison sniffled.

"This is really for Stephanie," Dad said. "It's her first wedding. It's a bigger deal for her. And her mother . . . well, you met Diane."

"Yeah," Madison said.

"She just likes things to be a certain way—her way—but that's okay. It's only for one weekend, right?" Dad said.

"I thought I was going to suffocate when she hugged me," Madison said.

Dad laughed.

"I mean it, Dad," Madison said, whispering so that no one else at the party would hear. "She's not normal."

"Maddie," Dad said. "Everyone's a little abnormal right now. You have to understand that. Stephanie, me, Diane, even you."

Madison swallowed hard. What was Dad talking about? How was Madison *abnormal*? Why was Dad getting his serious voice on? Didn't he know she needed him just to give her a hug and take her away from the party—now?

"I know this is a big weekend," Dad continued. "In more ways than one. And all these people can't help make it any easier or more comfortable. But even if I seem distracted, or Stephanie seems busy, we're here for you."

"Whatever," Madison said.

"Now, don't be that way," Dad said. "I hate it when you do that."

"What?" Madison said.

"I need you to try to behave, okay?" Dad pleaded. Madison felt as if he were talking to her the way he had when she was little.

"Behave?" Madison repeated. She was getting all choked up again.

"You know what I mean," Dad said, trying to soften his words. He kissed Madison on the forehead.

"I know," Madison said.

"I really want you to meet Stephanie's sisters. I know they're here somewhere. . . ." Dad scanned the crowd. "They're running the show, so I bet they are both in the back with Catering. . . ."

Madison rolled her eyes.

Dad knew what was wrong.

"I just need to mingle with a few more people. You sit here. Then we can head back to the hotel," he said. "I promise."

Madison wondered how Dad would ever be able to leave his own party. Was this just another promise that was made to be broken?

She stood up from the leather chair. "I'm coming with you," Madison said.

"You are?" Dad said.

Stephanie buzzed over toward them again. "Jeff, let's find the kids and Madison can hang out with them. You must be so bored by all these friends of my parents. . . ."

"Kids! That's a great idea!" Dad said.

Madison grabbed his arm. "I would rather be with *you*, Dad," she said.

Stephanie made a face. "You're sure?" she asked Madison.

"Yes," Madison said resolutely, staying by Dad's side.

Stephanie sighed. "All right."

"So, let's mingle," Dad said.

The three of them walked into the middle of the party action again. People rushed in to congratulate the bride and groom.

Across the room, Madison spotted the boy she had seen earlier and some other kids entering and exiting again. But she didn't make any move to introduce herself, and neither did they.

Instead, Madison clung to Dad as if he were a life preserver.

She wanted never to let go.

Chapter 10

Dad did make good on his promise to Madison—sort of.

After an hour of mingling, he and Madison headed back to the Bellville Villas and left Stephanie to party until the wee hours. Actually, most of the dinner guests ate and disappeared early, too. It wasn't a late, late night. Everyone was saving their energy for the main event on Saturday.

And that was still a whole day away.

Madison's heart sank when the attendant at the front desk of the Bellville Villas told them there were no messages from the Houston airport or Sky High Airlines. Madison was becoming more and more convinced that, indeed, her luggage had plummeted to earth somewhere north of nowhere.

She would never see her stuff again, she thought.

She and Dad took the elevator up to the third floor and said their good-nights. Dad thanked Madison for coming to the dinner, and then she thanked him for being such an understanding father "most of the time."

"I'm sorry about the way I acted at the party," Madison said as they stood in front of her room. She plugged her key card into the slot in the door and half hugged Dad good night at the same time.

"I don't ever want you to hide your feelings from me," Dad said. "Not even in the middle of my wed-ding."

"Okay." Madison nodded. "I won't."

She threw open the door.

"Hey, why is your light on?" Dad asked, curious. He pushed his way into the room ahead of her.

"I thought I turned it out. . . ." Madison said.

"Oh, no!" Dad cried. "Get in here, Maddie!"

Madison went inside.

There, on the bed, was a blue, checkered bag.

"My suitcase!" Madison shrieked when she saw it sitting in the middle of the bed. "It's *heeeeeeere*!"

Madison flung herself on top of the bag and unzipped the sides. Everything inside was intact, except for most of her clothes. Those, of course, were wrinkled beyond recognition.

"Well, you and your suitcase can get reacquain-ted," Dad said, opening the divider door that linked their two rooms. "I'm hitting the hay. But I'm right next door if you need me."

"Have a good sleep, Dad," Madison said.

Dad closed the door gently and disappeared into his room.

Madison felt as though she'd been shot full of electricity—or something just as powerful. Her bag was here! That made up for the bad party, the crowds of people, the stress—all of it. She picked through her clothes and pulled out her tried and true Lisa Simpson T-shirt that she often wore in place of pajamas. Then she pulled *off* the shorts and top she'd been wearing all day long.

"Ahhhh!" Madison said to herself when she'd finally washed her face and put on some clean clothes.

She sorted through some of her other outfits and collapsed onto the bed next to the hotel phone. The clock said nine-fifteen, which meant that it was after eleven back in Far Hills, but Madison picked up the phone and dialed anyway.

"Um . . . I'd like to make a collect call, please," she said into the receiver. "From Madison."

The operator put her on hold and asked her to wait until the party on the other end accepted the charges.

Madison sighed with relief when she heard the voice on the other end.

"Mom?" she said.

"Maddie?" Mom said with a yawn. "Where are you? Are you okay?"

"I'm just in the hotel, Mom. I had to talk to you," Madison said. "Are you asleep?"

"Yes. But don't worry. What's going on? How is Texas?" Mom asked.

Madison grunted into the phone. "Fine."

"Well!" Mom said. "That certainly doesn't sound too good."

Madison sighed into the phone. "Dad is fine. Stephanie is okay. But there are, like, a million people at this wedding, Mom. I don't know anyone. I am completely out of it."

"That is not true," Mom said. "You're one of the stars."

"Oh, Mom," Madison said.

"Phinnie misses you," Mom added. "Tonight, he went into your bedroom and curled up on top of your pillows. I think he must still smell you there."

"I miss him, too," Madison admitted.

There was silence on the phone.

"Mom?" Madison asked. "Can you get on the next plane and come here?"

Mom laughed. "Sure," she joked.

"I mean it," Madison said.

"What are you talking about?" Mom said. "Madison, trust me. This weekend will be over before you know it. And I know you will meet new people and have a lot of fun before it's done."

"Highly unlikely, Mom," Madison said.

"Well, you should try to meet people. Doesn't

Stephanie have a bunch of nieces and nephews your age?"

"I don't care," Madison said.

"Well, you should try," Mom said, trying to be encouraging. "Have you been practicing your reading for the wedding?"

Madison felt her cheeks get hot. She hadn't even *looked* at the book of poems in two days! It was packed in the suitcase that had spent the last day flying over Wisconsin.

"Sort of," Madison said. "I need to look at it again."

"Well, do that," Mom said. "And ask Stephanie if you can help her with anything around the wedding. Maybe she needs something. . . ."

"Why would she need me to help? She has a hundred other people to help her," Madison said.

"Sometimes it's good just to ask," Mom said.

"Okay, fine," Madison said. She was getting a little impatient. Her mom could hear it in her tone of voice.

"Now what's the matter?" Mom asked.

"It's just that—don't you feel strange at all about Dad getting married again?"

"Maddie, we've been through this. I am happy for Dad. He's happy. And it's natural for you to feel strange," Mom said.

"He's going to be different now," Madison said.

"What do you mean?" Mom asked softly.

"He's not going to have time for me or Phin anymore. He's going to be too busy with Stephanie," Madison said.

"Maddie," Mom said sweetly. "You have to stop worrying about Dad. He's not going anywhere. You need to believe that. You're not losing a father. . . ."

"Well, I'm not gaining a mother!" Madison snapped.

"I wasn't going to say that," Mom said.

"Sorry."

"Honey bear, maybe you should lie down and get some sleep," Mom suggested. "You sound tired."

"Yeah, I guess," Madison said. "And you should go to sleep, too."

"Why don't you call me tomorrow afternoon?" Mom asked.

Madison agreed to say good night and talk to her mom the next day. As soon as she hung up the phone, Madison realized she hadn't even told Mom about the lost suitcase.

Knock, knock, knock.

Madison glanced over at the adjoining door. What did Dad want? She lumbered over and unlocked the door from her side.

Madison was shocked to see Stephanie standing there, not Dad. She looked as though she had been crying.

"Hi there," Stephanie said, coming into the

room. "I just drove up from the ranch. I wanted to wish you good night, Maddie. We didn't really get a chance to talk tonight."

"Oh, that's okay," Madison said, feeling vaguely uncomfortable.

Stephanie blew her nose into a tissue and sniffled. Madison could see black mascara gummed up around her eyes.

"Thank you for coming to the party," Stephanie said. "I know how tough it was with all those people. Your dad said you were a little overwhelmed. I should have done a better job at introducing you around. . . ."

Madison sat and listened.

"As you saw, my family can be a lot to handle. Mother likes to do things big, like I told you. And this wedding has gotten to be very big, indeed. Maybe too big. But what can you do?"

Madison still didn't respond.

"Well, that was really all I wanted to say. . . ." Stephanie seemed uncomfortable now, too.

"It's really okay," Madison finally blurted out.

Stephanie smiled and took a deep breath. "What a big thing, getting married. I had no idea how complicated it could get."

Madison shrugged. "Me, neither."

"Your father says I get all worked up, and that I should just relax, but, you know, sometimes it's just hard not to get so emotional, and . . . well, I don't need to tell you all this, do I?" Stephanie bowed her head and sighed. "I talk too much."

They sat there in silence for a few minutes. Then Madison broke the silence.

"Stephanie?" Madison asked tentatively. "Do you love Dad?"

A look of shock spread over Stephanie's face. "Love him? Why, of course, I love him."

"I love him, too," Madison said. "I just wanted you to know that."

"Of course," Stephanie said. She looked deep into Madison's eyes. "You're a very special little girl," she said.

Madison hated the word "little," but she didn't voice her objection aloud.

"Thanks," Madison replied simply. "I guess."

"I'm lucky to have you *both* in my life," Stephanie said. "I am so excited about becoming your stepmother."

Madison hated that word, too. She couldn't help thinking of Cinderella. But she could also tell how hard Stephanie was trying to make nice with her. Madison reflected upon what Mom had said about asking if Stephanie needed help with the wedding.

"Um . . . is there anything I can do to help this weekend?" Madison asked. "Besides reading at the wedding, I mean."

Stephanie let out a little gasp. Then she started to cry again. Madison wasn't sure what to do.

"Are you okay?" Madison asked, her voice shaking a little.

"Oh! Oh!" Stephanie said. Real words seemed to have gotten trapped in her throat. "I'm just a little overwhelmed. Nothing for you to worry about." She wiped her eyes, which smudged the mascara some more.

Madison swallowed hard. This day rated right up there as one of the strangest days in her life. First, there had been the lost suitcase; then, the overpowering Texas heat; and now, *this*?

Madison thought about her friends back in Far Hills. She thought about Mom, sitting home alone with Phin. She thought about losing Dad . . . forever. And now, Stephanie was having a major meltdown. Seeing Stephanie cry made Madison want to cry. But she held it in.

"Are you sure you're okay?" Madison asked again.

"Maddie," Stephanie said, shaking off her tears. "I appreciate your offer to help, but there really isn't anything for you to do. I know that tomorrow my sisters will be running errands and that sort of thing. And you will get to meet all my nieces and nephews. I know they will love you. Who wouldn't love you?"

She leaned over and gave Madison a squeeze.

"Most of all, thank you for listening," Stephanie said. She stroked Madison's arm. "I hope you know that you can tell me anything, too."

Can I tell you that you make me nervous some-times and that I think you try too hard and that I really, really, really *don't want you to marry my dad?* Madison thought.

But of course, she said none of that out loud.

There was a loud bang on the divider door. Dad shouted through the partition, "Hey, what's going on in there? Slumber party?"

Madison rolled her eyes at Dad's lame attempt to be funny.

Stephanie stood up and went over to open the door. As she fiddled with the lock, Madison fell back-ward onto the bed and clutched at the pillows. The knot in the pit of her stomach had grown to the size of a watermelon.

"Madison Francesca Finn," Dad announced, com-ing into the room. He scooped Madison into his arms and gave her a big kiss.

Madison squirmed.

Stephanie crossed her arms and watched as Dad kissed Madison good night. "We'll finish talking later, okay?" she said.

Madison nodded.

"Have a good sleep, honey bear," Dad said. "Don't stay up watching T.V. all night. We have a big day tomorrow."

"Speaking of which," Stephanie said to Dad. "I need to get back on the road. Mother is expecting me back at the ranch tonight."

Madison forced a smile. "Good night," she said.

Stephanie and Dad disappeared through the divider door, locking it behind them with a loud click. Madison threw herself back onto the bed and reached for her laptop.

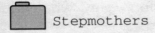 Stepmothers

I've only seen Stephanie cry once before and she didn't know I was looking. One night at Dad's apartment she was upset after dinner. But tonight she was a total mess. What am I supposed to say or do?

More than half the kids in my class at FHJH have divorced parents and most of those have stepparents. But I just am not ready to join that crowd. Why should I?

Now I know for sure: I hate Texas and everything about this weekend so far. I wish Phin was here so he would lick my toes and let me scratch his belly and then everything would be normal.

Then again, I'm not really sure what normal is anymore.

Rude Awakening: Do they call it "step" mother because it feels like this person wants to step all over everything and change my life?

Actually, they should call it stompmother.

Madison was just about to shut down her computer when she changed her mind and started a

new e-mail. She couldn't go to sleep without checking on someone.

```
From: MadFinn
To: Wetwinz
Subject: How r U?
Date: Thurs 18 July 10:49 PM
```

Just wanted to check up and see how
ur doing. Do you miss me b/c I miss
you guys A LOT! I was at this party
for Stephanie & my dad tonite and
felt like such a loser. Is it
possible to feel totally alone when
ur in a room with 300 people? Well,
not that many but close.

Thanks again for all ur amazing
ideas for the wedding collage. I
worked on it for most of the plane
ride since Dad was sleeping. And I
have all the stuff here tonite so I
can paste down flowers and work on
my poem as soon as I finish writing
this e-mail.

Which I guess is now. See ya.

Love,

Maddie

Madison glanced over at a bag of paper she'd tucked between the bed and the end table. Collage materials were bursting out of the side. Madison was lucky that neither Stephanie nor Dad had noticed it.

She leaned over, dragged the paper, ribbon, and glue onto the bed, and clicked the television on.

There was still a lot of work to be done for her project—and no time to do it. Stretching across the bed, Madison tried to work on her wedding poem. But all she was able to do was scribble lines across the page.

After everything that had happened that night, it was hard to get into the mood to write a bunch of flowery, happy stuff about Dad and Stephanie.

Really hard.

Madison rested her head on her hands and stared at the T.V. She clicked the channels but couldn't find anything to watch. After a while, the voices and music seemed to melt together.

Her eyelids felt heavy.

Within ten minutes, Madison was asleep.

Chapter 11

Knock, knock, knock.

Madison thought she was dreaming until she heard Dad's voice.

"Madison! Madison!" he called out through the divider door. "Are you awake?"

Groggily, Madison opened her eyes. She had fallen asleep facedown on top of her collage materials. Her arms had lines and indentations on them from where she had pressed against the paper and ribbons.

And her hair looked like a bird's nest.

"Maddie!" Dad called again. "Are you decent?"

"Dad? Hold on!" Madison said, blinking twice and leaping up from the bed. Panicked, she stuffed the collage materials under the bed and quickly yanked the blankets down. "Come in!" she called out, sticking her nose under the blanket.

Dad burst through the door. "You're still in *bed*?" he asked.

Madison glanced at the clock for the first time. She hadn't realized how late it was.

"Whoops," she mumbled. "I guess I'd better get ready."

Dad looked sweaty, even though the air-conditioning was on full blast in the hotel room.

"Hurry up, okay?" he asked Madison, running his fingers through his hair.

Madison smiled sweetly and jumped out from under the covers. "Okay!" she declared, throwing her arms around Dad's waist.

Dad let down his guard with a sigh. "I can't believe I'm getting married tomorrow," he said.

"Me, neither," Madison said.

"Stephanie looked pretty last night, don't you think?" Dad asked with a twinkle in his eye.

Madison nodded. "I guess so. When she wasn't crying."

"She's just so nervous, that's all," Dad explained. "I am, too."

Dad glanced over at the table in Madison's hotel room. On top was the copy of the book of love poems Dad and Stephanie had given her for the reading. Dad pointed to it.

"Been practicing?" he asked.

Madison felt all the color drain out of her cheeks. She hadn't opened it since they had gotten to the hotel.

"I was looking at it last night," Madison said.

"Shakespeare is hard to read," Dad said.

Madison's heart was beating fast.

The minute Dad left the room, she would open the book and start reading. . . .

"Well, I better go shave and call Stephanie's sister. She's coming for us," Dad said, planting a kiss on Madison's head. "I will be back in about thirty minutes."

Madison breathed a sigh of relief when Dad returned to his own room. She quickly gathered together her collage pieces from under the bed and headed to the bathroom for a shower.

She decided the best thing to wear was Fiona's purple sundress. That way she could keep cool—and keep connected to her BFF at the same time. Madison didn't know how the day would turn out. She worried that Stephanie's nieces and nephews wouldn't like her. Or maybe *she* wouldn't like them. Either way, Madison hoped the dress would do her some good.

Luckily, the dress was a perfect fit. And she'd remembered to pack her purple barrettes at the last minute. Although black sandals didn't completely pull the whole outfit together, they still went with almost everything, so Madison pulled them on. Strawberry-kiwi lip gloss came last.

"I wish Hart could see me like this," Madison thought to herself, puckering her lips in the mirror. It felt odd to look and feel good after falling asleep on top of a pile of papers in a strange hotel miles from home.

"Wahoo!" Dad let out a holler and barged right back into Madison's room.

She jumped, startled.

"Dad! What are you doing?"

Dad grinned. "Getting in gear, my dear!" he chirped in his best Texas twang. "I was dragging a little, but now I've decided to be worry-free. And don't you look pah-retty?"

"Oh, Dad!" Madison put her hands on her hips. "Don't talk like that," she said.

"Ready to hit the road?" Dad asked in his normal voice.

Madison nodded. She grabbed her orange bag and headed for the door. Even though it was bulky, and she probably didn't need half of the stuff inside, she didn't want to be separated from it.

In the elevator, Dad couldn't stop bouncing around. He started out humming. As the elevator beeped at each floor, he made his own beeping noises.

"Dad!" Madison groaned, rolling her eyes. "What is your problem?"

He laughed. "I told you. I woke up nervous. But I'm working on it."

Madison couldn't believe this was what Dad was like when he was nervous. Why couldn't he bite his nails or do something else, *silently*?

"Dad, I hate to tell you this, but no one beeps when they're nervous," Madison said.

"Oh, really?" Dad chuckled. "Good thing you told me that."

Madison sneered a fake-o sneer. "You are *so* embarrassing, sometimes."

The elevator doors opened onto the hotel lobby, which was bustling with hotel staff and guests and luggage carts. Madison and her dad squeezed through a crowd of people, who Madison guessed were part of a tour group, because they all had cameras around their necks.

"I didn't know Bellville was a tourist spot," Dad said as they walked away. "Then again, maybe they're all wedding guests. Ha!"

Madison laughed at that one. She knew that Dad felt the same way she did about the number of people that seemed to be participating in the Wolfe and Finn wedding. Namely, that it was *too large*.

Outside in the parking lot, Madison met Stephanie's sister Wanda for the first time. She had been assigned to driving duty for the morning and was escorting them to breakfast at a local restaurant.

145

The first thing Madison noticed about Wanda was her hair.

It was big. And in the Texas morning sun, it looked pink, which matched her head-to-toe pink ensemble.

"Golly, I didn't have much of a chance to talk last night," Wanda said to Dad, swatting at his arm with a little laugh. "And I didn't meet *you* at all!"

Wanda gently touched Madison's shoulder. "You are as pretty as a picture," Wanda said. "Just like Stephanie always says. 'Course, I have seen your picture dozens of times. And where did you ever get that darling little dress! My Tiffany would just *loooooove* that!"

Madison tugged at her dress. "Thanks," she said.

"Shall we hit the road?" Dad suggested, putting his arm around Wanda with a gentle nudge.

Madison could tell he was itching to start his day-before-the-big-day.

The leather seats inside Wanda's car felt like ice cubes. Madison guessed they were permanently chilled from having the air-conditioning on all the time. The cool car was better than the Texas heat, but Madison was relieved that she didn't have to sit there for very long. The drive over to Monica's Café for breakfast passed quickly.

Monica's didn't look like much from the road, but inside, the café was filled with pots of colored

146

flowers and brightly colored tablecloths. Stephanie still had not arrived, but most of her family was there already, sipping coffee and orange juice. The dining tables were arranged in a horseshoe pattern on a glassed-in terrace.

"I promise I won't run off," Dad said, squeezing Madison's hand as they entered the restaurant. "Let me introduce you to a few people."

Madison smoothed out the skirt on Fiona's dress and took a deep breath.

Across the restaurant, she saw a group of girls talking together. They looked to be just about Madison's age; they didn't wave hello. One girl with long, blond hair looked right at Madison and then turned to whisper to another girl.

They reminded Madison of some other people she knew.

Poison Ivy and her drones.

"Maddie, I'd like you to meet Stephanie's other sister, Bethany," Dad said, turning Madison around to face a strange woman with cropped brown hair. She wore big, clunky earrings and too much make-up, but she didn't stop smiling once, the whole time Madison talked to her.

"Madison Finn!" Bethany proclaimed. "Well, it's about time, Jeff!"

Madison wondered how she had missed meeting all these people the night before. Everything was a bit of a blur.

"Nice to meet you," Madison said, extending her hand to shake Bethany's hand.

"Oh, Jeff," Bethany whispered to Dad. "She's a plum."

Dad rubbed Madison's back as if to say, "Hang in there, honey bear. I'm right here."

Madison glanced around the room in search of other familiar faces.

That was when she saw him.

Across the room.

Smiling.

Madison looked away.

"Can we go over here?" Madison asked Dad, yanking on his arm and trying desperately to turn away from the boy.

"Hey!" Dad cried. "Wait a minute! I want to introduce you to some of Stephanie's nieces and nephews. . . ."

Madison's throat closed up for a moment. She knew what—or who—Dad was talking about.

"Kirk!" Dad called out loud. "Get over here!"

Dad was all smiles as he introduced Madison to Kirk Smith, who was Stephanie's sister Bethany's son—and who was also the boy who had smiled at Madison.

Kirk shrugged and said hello to Madison, half smiling. His eyes crinkled up, and he shoved his hands into his shorts pockets.

"What's up?" Kirk said.

"Up? Not much," Madison replied, as if she were speaking a different language.

"Kirk, we wanted you to meet Maddie back in Far Hills, remember?"

"Sure," Kirk said. "I remember."

"Sorry about that," Madison said.

"No biggie," Kirk said. "Hey, want to meet some of the other cousins? There's a bunch of us just hanging out on the patio."

Madison looked to Dad for approval. Dad gave her his blessing with a wink. "Go have a good time," Dad said.

Madison bravely followed Kirk out onto the patio. It was hard to resist a cuter-than-cute guy under these circumstances, Madison told herself, even if he was fourteen—almost two years older than she was. She considered whether maybe (just maybe) Kirk was cuter than Hart.

As they stepped outside, Madison spotted the Poison Ivy clone, sitting on a low wall with a bunch of other girls. Kirk walked over with Madison.

"Hey, Tiff," Kirk said. "This is Madison. Um, Madison . . . this is Tiffany."

Tiffany flipped her hair—just like Ivy—and then smiled wide, as if she were acting in a toothpaste commercial.

"Hiya," Tiffany said. "So, now we're all going to be cousins, huh?"

Madison swallowed hard. "I guess."

Mr. and Mrs. Wolfe made some announcements, and breakfast was finally served. All the kids meandered inside. Most of the boys rushed on ahead of Madison, and Tiffany and the other girls stuck together.

Only Kirk hung back to talk.

"Thanks for being so nice to me," Madison told him. "This is all so . . ."

"Insane!" Kirk laughed. "My family is, like . . . really strange, I know."

Madison giggled. "Well, I wasn't going to say that."

"It's okay, I'm used to it. Me and Tiff always say that they should do a reality T.V. show about the Wolfe family," Kirk said. "Not that I'd be caught watching it."

Me and Tiff?

Madison couldn't understand how Kirk and Tiffany could be so close, but Kirk made it sound as if they were more best pals than cousins.

Breakfast was displayed on yet another gigantic buffet featuring an ice sculpture shaped like the state of Texas. Kirk pointed to it and laughed.

"Grandma Diane always puts out these freaky ice molds shaped like Texas and cowboy boots, and I'm, like, 'Whoa!'" Kirk said dramatically.

Madison pointed to the spread of food on the table. "Is that steak? For breakfast?"

"Are you kidding?" Kirk said. "My family raises their own cattle. We always have steak, at every meal."

Madison thought it was funny how Dad could first marry Mom, a total vegetarian, and then marry someone who was so into beef.

"Maddie!" Stephanie ran over and threw her arms around Madison. She leaned in and whispered, "Sorry about last night. I was upset."

"That's okay," Madison said.

"Aunt Steph!" Kirk said, leaning over to give Stephanie a kiss hello. Before she could make contact, he leaned away. "Gotcha!"

Stephanie chuckled. "Watch it, buster!" she said. "What other trouble are you getting into around here?"

"You know. The usual," Kirk said.

Madison swooned when Kirk smiled. What was she thinking? This guy was *definitely* cuter than Hart.

"Well, be good," Stephanie cautioned him. "This is my wedding, after all."

"Whatever you say, Aunt Steph," Kirk said.

"Oh, you're trouble!" Stephanie said. "Madison, keep an eye on him for me, will you?"

Madison felt a major blush coming on, although Kirk didn't seem to notice—or care.

"Hey, let's get some grub and sit with Tiff," he suggested.

They got their plates of food and moved to sit near the rest of the cousins. Madison would have preferred a quiet table for two, but this would have to do instead.

Throughout the breakfast, everyone chatted about people and places Madison had never heard about. She was definitely the out-of-towner in this crowd. Tiff smiled a few times, but other than that she was absolutely Ivy-ish, acting as though she knew everything and talking more than everyone else.

Unfortunately, Madison was stuck with Tiff and her crew. And after the meal, Dad needed to go with "the boys" to a local shop, where his rented tuxedo was being held for him. He and Madison would be separated once again.

Dad already owned a tux, but it had been worn once before—at his first wedding. So wearing it to wedding number two had not seemed to him like a very good idea. Dad was as superstitious as Madison was.

So, while Dad went off to Mostly Formals, Madison was thrown to the Wolfes for the afternoon. Once again she got stuck with Stephanie's sister Wanda, who wanted to go shopping in Bellville. This time, Wanda was accompanied by a cousin of hers named Marly, a soft-spoken woman with glasses who talked barely above a whisper.

Madison thought about shopping for hours with total strangers. That didn't sound very fun.

Maybe Wanda wouldn't have to shop? Madison had some lucky things in her favor.

Lucky thing number one: Wanda's daughter, Tiffany, would *not* be joining them. Instead of shopping, Tiff was headed back to the ranch with her grandmother to help decorate. Madison had not been asked back to the ranch. She wasn't, of course, offended. Right now, the last place she wanted to be was stuck in a room decorating the walls with crepe paper, in the company of Miss Texas Poison Ivy.

Lucky thing number two: Wanda's shopping route took her right past the Bellville Villas. That route gave Madison a brilliant escape-from-the-shopping-trip idea. She would politely ask to be dropped off at her hotel room so she could wait there until Wanda and Marly finished their shopping. That way, Madison could check her e-mail, work on her wedding collage, and avoid Wanda at all costs. To make the plan sound *really* good, Madison embellished it with a few white lies.

"Um . . . Wanda . . . I'm feeling kind of tired. . . . Well, actually, I have a stomachache. . . . Well, actually, it's more like a headache. . . ."

"You're sick?" Wanda exclaimed. "Good Lord. Let me feel your forehead."

"Gee," Madison said, extending her lie. "Since we're so close to the hotel, do you think maybe I could stop in and take a nap while you shop?"

"Stop?" Wanda asked. She didn't warm up to the

153

idea right away. "Hmph. I just don't know. I feel funny leaving you alone. . . ."

"Oh, Wanda, I'm sure Madison can take care of herself," Marly chimed in. "And she should rest if she doesn't feel well. Today's a big day."

Madison nodded at Marly, feeling a momentary bond, but Wanda still seemed concerned.

"I just don't know, Madison. Your daddy might not like this," she said. "You promise me you'll stay there till we come back, right?"

"Of course, I will!" Madison said. "I'm just going right up to the room to lie down. . . ."

"Wanda, let her go," Marly said softly.

"Well, shoot," Wanda said with a wink. "I guess I don't need to be worried. You're a big girl, aren't you?"

Madison grinned. Finally, *someone* thought so.

"Let's just walk you up there," Wanda said as she parked the car. She entered the lobby with Madison and boarded the elevator for the third floor.

Madison promised to lock the door and not open it up for anyone.

"We'll see you in a flash," Wanda promised. "I'll call when we're heading back, 'kay?"

Madison nodded and closed the door behind Wanda.

"Success!" she thought as she jumped onto the bed. The hotel room was cool, and Madison pulled a blanket over her. She glanced over at the phone to see if maybe someone had called, but there was no blinking light. No messages.

Madison pulled the green leather book of love poems on to her lap and opened it to the page of her special sonnet. It was time to practice for real! The rehearsal was only hours away.

Madison read through the sonnet once, twice, four times. How could she have waited so long to practice? After her sixth read-through, Madison felt comfortable with it. She could do this, she told herself. It wasn't as if she had to memorize it. That would have been a disaster.

After setting the book aside, Madison had plenty of time left before Wanda and Marly returned. So she powered up her laptop. Online, Madison discovered a message, sent very early that morning, from Aimee. It had been marked with a red exclamation point, meaning "urgent." Aimee never added exclamation points.

Madison clicked on it immediately.

```
From: Balletgrl
To: MadFinn
Subject: Fiona's Dad
Date: Fri 19 July 9:03 AM
```
Oh Maddie I left a message @ ur house this morning, b/c the worst thing ever happened late last nite-- and I couldn't get ur mom on the

phone. Fiona's Dad had a major heart attack. I guess he tried to lift something and had this mega-attack. It was all so sudden. Everyone in Far Hills is talking about it. And everyone is soooooo worried about him. He's in the part of the hospital called ICU I think that's intense care unit.

Of course, Fiona is very sad. I only talked 2 her for a minute this morning from the hospital b/c she called me 2 tell me what happened. She was crying so hard. I felt awful. Fiona and her dad r sooooo close.

I really wanted to tell u right away b/c I know u would want to call her yourself and all that. What are you supposed to say when this happens? I think (I hope) he will be ok but I dunno. It seems dumb to say "don't worry" when OF COURSE Fiona should worry. What do you think, Maddie?

I miss you more than n e thing and I really, really wish u could be here RTVM! Then we could go cheer

up Fiona <u>together</u> like real BFFs.
Write back or even call me @ home,
ok? This is the worst day ever
seeing my friend so sad.

Love ya, Aim

Madison stared at the screen. She reread Aimee's words. And then she started to cry.

Chapter 12

As soon as she'd read the news, Madison tried calling Fiona on the hotel phone, but she was able to reach only the Waterses' answering machine. Madison guessed that everyone must have been at Far Hills Hospital. She tried calling Aimee, too, but no one was home there, either. Even Madison's own mom was out.

So there she sat, Madison Francesca Finn, stranded in a chilly hotel room in the middle of Texas, separated from her neurotic dad, who was getting married to someone Madison wasn't even sure she liked anymore, and worrying about her BFF, whose dad had just had a heart attack.

It was hard not to keep on crying.

As a last resort, to talk to *someone*, Madison went online again.

Surprise!

Madison couldn't believe it. Fiona was online—right now! How was that possible?

She Insta-Messaged her BFF.

```
<MadFinn>: What r u doing online????
<Wetwinz>: Maddie! I was just
   thinking of u
<MadFinn>: are u @ home?
<Wetwinz>: no @ the hospital
<MadFinn>: aim told me everything I
   think it's so awful OH FIONA
<Wetwinz>: Dad was in emergency
   surgery b4 but he's in recovery
   now and we're all waiting 2 talk
   2 the doc so mom told me I should
   keep busy. That's y im on the
   computer since this hospital has
   a library they let some people
   use the terminals with special
   permission
<MadFinn>: r u ok?
<Wetwinz>: not really I dunno I was
   there when it happened Daddy
   was in the kitchen and dropped
   a stack of plates from the
   dishwasher and then he just fell
   to the floor Chet called 911 and
   my mom was in the other room she
   ran in it happened fast
<MadFinn>: that's awful
```

```
<Wetwinz>: I thought the worst, you
   know?
<MadFinn>: oh fiona
<Wetwinz>: I mean he's ok now (I
   hope) but this has been such a
   strange week none of us thought
   he would be the one to have a
   heart attack that sounds so scary
   doesn't it?
<MadFinn>: I wish I could be
   there w/u
<Wetwinz>: me 2 I could use one of
   ur hugs
<MadFinn>: <:>)
```

All at once, Madison and Fiona's conversation online was interrupted by another Insta-Message. *Aimee!*

```
<Balletgrl>: OMG r u really both
   online????
```

The three friends agreed to meet in a private chat room called FRNDLY.

```
<Balletgrl>: I knew you'd be online
   fiona b/c we said we'd talk 18r
   but maddie it is sooooo awesome
   that u r 2
<MadFinn>: yeah
```

\<Balletgrl\>: how's ur Dad, Fiona??
\<Wetwinz\>: I was just tellin maddie
    that he's better I think mom is
    checking him out in a while and
    she told Chet to go home and
    sleep we're all pretty tired so
    he went back to the house with my
    Gramps
\<MadFinn\>: ur whole family is there?
\<Wetwinz\>: pretty much so. everyone
    is supportive but nothing like
    friends right?
\<MadFinn\>: I'm sorry I'm not
    there!!
\<Balletgrl\>: being online is
    practically as good as being next
    door, right?
\<MadFinn\>: so ur Dad is in
    intensive care right now?
\<Wetwinz\>: yes but can we talk
    about something else?
\<MadFinn\>: I'm sorry
\<Wetwinz\>: no dnt be I just feel
    weird I wanna stop thinking about
    him can u talk about something
    else please Maddie, tell us about
    Texas
\<MadFinn\>: OH don't ask me!
\<Balletgrl\>: Y not?
\<MadFinn\>: for 1 thing right now
    I'm ALONE in my hotel and my dad

is off getting a tuxedo and I'm supposed 2 go 2 this TEA PARTY later gack!!!

<Wetwinz>: a tea party?

<Balletgrl>: WAYTA?

<MadFinn>: they have all these fancy parties and there's this girl here who reminds me of Ivy oh she is sooooo fake

<Balletgrl>: Maybe it's Ivy in disguise sent to torture you

<MadFinn>: VVF

<Wetwinz>: are there a lotta wedding guests?

<MadFinn>: a bazillion and they are all from Texas I feel like such an outsider

<Wetwinz>: bummer

<Balletgrl>: n e cute guys??? HA

<MadFinn>: well

<Balletgrl>: fess up

<MadFinn>: there is one, sorta

<Balletgrl>: no way!!!

<MadFinn>: yeah way, his name is Kirk and he's 14 actually ;-o

<Wetwinz>: kirk sounds like a QT

<Balletgrl>: what does he look like

<MadFinn>: brownish blond hair and tall he dresses really cool and he talks with this cute accent

162

<Balletgrl>: maybe u can fall in
    love there
<MadFinn>: YR--he's my cousin-to-be
    so how r the guys @ home?
<Wetwinz>: this morning everyone
    came over and brought flowers for
    mom, me & chet, isn't that the
    sweetest
<Balletgrl>: OMG drew has this
    suntan and he looks soooo happy
    now that he's with that girl
    Elaine I never thought he was
    cute b4 but I have changed my
    mind big time
<MadFinn>: really? drew is actually
    going OUT w/someone?
<Wetwinz>: that's not true Aim, he's
    not dating her
<Balletgrl>: well it's close enough
    and like I said he looks more
    like a hottie now unlike b4
<Wetwinz>: he isn't THAT cute and
    besides egg is cuter
<Balletgrl>: what-EVER
<MadFinn>: how about Hart?
<Wetwinz>: he's the same I guess
<MadFinn>: who is he hanging with?
<Balletgrl>: y do u care, maddie?
<Wetwinz>: do u like him or
    something?
<Balletgrl>: yeah remember u were

```
checking hart out @ the bookstore
the other day I knew it
```

Madison's fingers froze on the keyboard. She couldn't let her friends figure out that she really *did* have a crush on Hart! She had to make something up—fast.

Angry denial was too obvious. Madison went for a distraction tactic instead.

```
<MadFinn>: wait--did I tell u that
    this guy Kirk in Texas asked
    me to dance w/him at the
    wedding?
```

Madison couldn't believe her the speed of her lie. She swallowed hard and hoped that Fiona and Aimee would stop asking questions about Hart.

```
<Balletgrl>: dance? get out!!! That
    is so great!
<Wetwinz>: u HAVE to take a pic so
    we can see
```

Madison breathed a sigh of relief.
She talked more about the Texas heat. . . .
She listed the special events that had been planned for the wedding. . . .
She updated her friends on the so-so progress of the wedding collage. . . .

But all of a sudden, Fiona interrupted with the news that she had to get offline immediately. She needed to go and meet with her family. The doctors were coming back with news about her dad.

Madison stopped chatting. Talk of boys suddenly seemed unimportant, compared to the serious issues that Fiona was dealing with.

```
<Wetwinz>: I promise I'll e you
   guys any newz from here once I C
   my dad in person
<MadFinn>: hope evrything is ok
<Wetwinz>: GL @ the wedding
<Balletgrl>: I so wish we were all
   together right now!
<MadFinn>: me 2 :>(
<Wetwinz>: gotta run--xoxoxxoxox
<Balletgrl>: BFN
<Wetwinz>: *poof*
<MadFinn>: BYE ILYG!!!!!
```

After saying her sudden good-byes to Aimee and Fiona, Madison was pleasantly surprised to find two e-mails waiting for her.

```
From: Bigwheels
To: MadFinn
Subject: Re: We're Heeeeere
Date: Fri 19 July 10:11 AM
```
I just realized when I was writing

this that since ur in Texas now we're CLOSER--now ur only an hour away instead of 3 hours. Cool, huh? It must be so hot there. It's hot here, too, but only in the 80s, not almost 100. Is it hot in Far Hills, too? My dad sez the whole country is having a heat wave. I hope by now u got ur suitcase. It would look pretty weird wearing shorts to the wedding, right?

What is a "girl" day? Where's ur Dad? Are there any other relatives there or is it all ur stepmom--I mean FUTURE stepmom--and her family? I hate being around a bunch of new people and having to talk and act nice when I feel uncomfortable. You know what I mean?

I am babysitting my bro & sis BTW, but my mom isn't paying me. I decided it was ok b/c mom and dad promised me that if I'm good @ it they'll get me MY OWN laptop computer at the end of the summer. Can u believe that? Then we can e-mail ALL THE TIME. Well, more than we do now.
How's the wedding collage? I bet ur

still working on it! LOL. I
attached some clip art and a poem I
found about love. It's goofy but
maybe it will give u more ideas.
See whatcha think.

And write back soon. I want to hear
EVERYTHING.

Yours till the chili dogs,

Bigwheels aka Vicki

<attachment>: love will keep us
(poem)

Madison grinned and hit SAVE. She would respond
to Bigwheels later—when there was more time to
think and when she'd had a chance to go through
the poem attachment.
She clicked on the next message.

From: ff_budgefilms
To: MadFinn
Subject: Phinnie Misses You
Date: Fri 19 July 11:01 AM

Bark! The two of us are sitting
here in my office and it just isn't
the same around here, honey bear.
We don't like it when you're away!
I hope the wedding weekend is going

well. I'm sure your dad is taking good care of you. Be good to him, too. I can't wait to see pictures of you in that orange dress!

We'll talk on the phone today or tomorrow, okay?

Just know that I love you very much.

Love,

Mom

p.s. I am sure you have heard about Fiona's father. I am sending flowers from all of us with get-well wishes. I know he will be fine so don't worry. Take care.

Madison couldn't believe what difference two e-mails could make, but they did make a difference. And she hadn't even gotten any junk e-mail, either! *That* was a first.

Brrrrrrrrrrrrring-a-ding!

The hotel phone rang. Madison nearly jumped off the bed. She flung the blanket off and picked up the receiver before the second ring.

"Hello?"

"Well darlin'," the voice on the other end said in a deep, Texas drawl.

It was Wanda.

"You won't believe this, Madison, but my car broke down. Marly and I are here at the gas station waiting for the mechanic. Of all the crazy things that could happen, wouldn't you know it? Just my luck!"

"So . . . are we still going to the tea party?" Madison asked.

"Well, shoot!" Wanda said. "'Course! We're just going to stick around here for a short spell and see if they can fix my brake. Chances are someone else will come in the van and get all of us and haul us back to the ranch, 'kay?"

"Okay," Madison said in her most agreeable voice.

"You just sit tight, sweetie. Marly and I will call you in a bit," Wanda said.

As Madison hung up the phone, she wondered where Dad was right now. He would probably freak out if he knew she'd spent half the morning holed up in the air-conditioned hotel room. He'd be worried.

At the same time, she couldn't believe her continuing luck.

Not only had she had time to contact her BFFs, Mom, *and* Bigwheels. Now, she even had *extra* time to work on another page of her wedding collage.

DREAMS

Celebrate

WOOF!

LOVE

Forever

Thanks for taking me for walks. I'm excited about having a stepmom, too. Love, Phinnie

Chapter 13

 The Bellville Tea Party

I have only been to one tea party in my life, in second grade, and there were dolls involved. Today's wedding tea party was nothing like that. Here's what a girl day is: a bunch of ladies sitting around talking about flowers and dresses. I love girl stuff too, but I was so BORED!

Not only that, but Stephanie was too busy to really talk to me. And then everyone started talking about the wedding gifts they got Dad and Stephanie. I couldn't believe the things people were buying like crystal bells and big, huge things that have to be shipped separately.

Here I am, barely able to finish one dumb collage. Who wants a piece of paper with pictures and words stuck to it when you can have a life-size crystal collie or a complete set of silver serving pieces with little lassos on the end?

To make matters worse, Tiffany and her cousins were all dressed in these perfect outfits with matching sandals. I thought my purple dress looked okay, but my black sandals didn't really match so well. For the rehearsal dinner tonight I'm wearing Aimee's white skirt with embroidered red flowers and a peasant blouse. I don't know what I'd do if I hadn't borrowed clothes from my BFFs. They are lifesavers.

Today my cousin-to-be Tiffany told me she has a stylist coming to her HOUSE to do her hair for the wedding! It made me think of myself, trying to French-braid my hair alone in the hotel bathroom. Actually, I counted and Tiffany flipped her hair every ten minutes today. Could anything be more annoying?

Rude Awakening: Whoever said it's better to feel good than to look good never went to a Wolfe tea party in Bellville, Texas.

Even though the wedding parties are the main things driving me crazy, I think I'm feeling sadder than sad right now b/c I found out my friend Fiona's Dad had a heart attack. Is that possible? He wasn't even sick! I haven't seen my dad since I heard the news. He's been gone all day doing "guy" wedding stuff. Apparently, Dad got his tux this morning and went fly-fishing or wade fishing all afternoon. I don't even know what that is. But I should just shut up. I can't rip everything apart. I've only been here a day.

I just miss Dad. A lot.

I wish he were here so I could tell him I love him.

"Hey! Maddie!" It was Dad, banging on the divider door between their rooms with his fist.

"Oh, Dad! Wait a sec!" Madison said. But before she could close her laptop, Dad flew in through the divider door with his arms wide open.

"I need a Madison hug right now! Right now!" Dad said, as if he were psychic and had heard Madison's secret, typed-in wish.

"Oh, Dad! I'm so happy to see you!" Madison giggled. She closed the notebook and gave him the hug he wanted.

"What a day! I caught a largemouth bass, rented a tux, met about thirty members of the Wolfe family I never knew existed. Better than an Indiana Jones adventure, right?" Dad said, winking at Madison.

Madison laughed along with Dad, but only for a second. Then she got serious.

"Dad," Madison said. "I heard really bad news today. Fiona's dad had a heart attack."

173

"What!" Dad exclaimed. He looked stunned. "Oh, no! What happened?"

"I guess he just got chest cramps and collapsed. Something like that," Madison said. "He wasn't sick or anything."

"Oh, that's awful news," Dad said, sitting on the edge of the bed. "How are Mrs. Waters and Chet?"

"I don't know, Dad," Madison said, her voice a little shaky. She sat next to Dad. "I think I feel sick."

"Oh, Maddie," Dad said. He grabbed Madison and gave her another hug. "Honey, I'm sure Mr. Waters will be okay. I know it."

"I guess," Madison said. She felt tears welling up and swallowed hard so she wouldn't cry. "I just wish I'd been fishing with you today, or spent some time with you today. That's all. When I heard about Fiona's dad, I felt worried about you. Does that make any sense?"

"Oh, Maddie, I am sorry you had to spend so much time alone. I'm sorry you got stuck with Wanda and Marly," Dad said.

"Dad," Madison said, looking away. "This whole trip to Texas is just too . . . too . . . much."

Dad stroked the top of Madison's head. "I know. I never expected that in two weeks someone could pull together a wedding this crazy. I really did think it was going to be much smaller. Leave it to Stephanie's mom. . . ."

Madison just rolled her eyes, but Dad saw her do it.

"Aw, we've been over this. She means well, Maddie," Dad said with a frown.

"Yeah, I know," Madison said. "But does she always have to be so touchy-feely?" She bit her lip so she wouldn't say anything else that was negative.

"That is such awful news about Mr. Waters," Dad said, getting back on topic. He wrapped his arm around Madison. "Are you okay? Do you need anything? What can I do?"

"Well . . . can we just hang out for the rest of the night and get room service, just the two of us?" Madison asked. "Can we spend some more time alone together before you and Stephanie get married?"

Dad bowed his head. "Oh, Maddie . . ."

"I know! You don't have to say it," Madison said. "We can't."

"You'll have me all to yourself when we get home to Far Hills," Dad said.

"But what if *you* have a heart attack?" Madison asked.

"Oh, Maddie," Dad said gently. "I'm not planning on it. Don't worry yourself about that."

"But it could happen?" Madison asked, throwing her arms back around her dad.

"I'll be fine, Maddie," Dad said again. "I love you so much."

Madison stood up and went to look at herself in the mirror above the dresser. Dad followed her. He looked at Madison in the mirror while she wiped the tears away.

"You haven't even told me," Dad asked. "How do I look?"

"Good," Madison said.

"You look good, too," Dad said. He turned Madison around and pulled her into his arms. "You'll be the belle of the ball."

"Stop it, Dad," Madison said.

"I especially like your hair," Dad added. Madison had worn it loose with a braided headband. "You hardly ever wear it down like that. And you're wearing the moonstone earrings I gave to you. Yes, you look very pretty tonight."

"Oh, Dad!" Madison said, now feeling one hundred percent embarrassed. Dad always said the right things—nice things—but sometimes they made her feel self-conscious. "Thanks, Dad."

"Thank *you*," Dad said as they prepared to leave the hotel room and head downstairs. One of Stephanie's old friends, who lived in downtown Bellville, was coming by the hotel to pick them up.

"Thank me for what?" Madison asked.

"For being you. For being here. For lots of things," Dad said.

"I feel better now," Madison admitted.

"I want you to have a good time tonight, okay?"

Dad said. "Better than last night. Try to give this place and the other people here a chance."

"I will," Madison reassured him.

"Good answer!" Dad said, giving her a peck on the cheek. He smelled like lime aftershave lotion.

As they walked out of the room, Madison grabbed the little straw bag with embroidered flowers that matched her skirt; and slid the green leather book of poems inside it.

She couldn't help wondering what outfits Tiffany and the others would be wearing.

The ride to the Wolfe ranch took longer than it should have.

Dad sweated it out in the front seat.

"What's with the traffic?" he asked, about a dozen times. They were already more than a half hour late.

Stephanie's friend Mike, who had picked them up at the hotel, seemed unfazed by the delay. He tried to engage Dad in some friendly talk about sports or stocks or one of those things that Madison couldn't have cared less about.

Meanwhile, Madison sat staring through the backseat window, already plotting how and where she would hide from the crowds at this next Wolfe event. She opened up the book of poems and read her selection silently to herself.

As they pulled up to the ranch, Madison spotted

the already-familiar faces of the staff members who parked cars. Giant flower arrangements decorated the front entryway of the main house. Every time they came to the ranch it seemed *bigger.*

Stephanie's mother was out front, greeting guests with her painted-on red lips and mile-wide smile.

"Jeff!" Mrs. Wolfe screeched when Dad opened the door of Mike's car and piled out, shaking the wrinkles out of his suit jacket and wiping a little per-spiration off his forehead. "Where on earth have you *beeeeen?*"

Madison could see Dad's shoulders slump. "We stopped for a bite on the way," he joked.

Mrs. Wolfe looked appalled.

"Do you think it's funny, Jeffrey?" she said, tsk-tsking Dad with a wave of her well-manicured fingertip. "I've got guests waiting. . . ."

Just then, Stephanie appeared at the top of the steps.

"Jeff!" she cried, running to greet Dad with a big embrace. She looked over Dad's shoulder and waved at Madison. "I guess Mother told you we were wor-ried about you three."

Stephanie reached out to give Mike a hello, too. He kissed her on the cheek and headed inside.

"Sorry. We hit some traffic," Dad said, stuttering a little as he tried to explain. "Mike was driving as fast as he could."

"Oh, don't worry," Stephanie started to say.

"Hmmmph!" Mrs. Wolfe said. Despite Dad's detailed explanation, she still looked unhappy. "Well, I'm a little worried myself. We'd better get in there, Stephanie Mae, or else the whole schedule tonight will be torn to bits."

Madison watched Mrs. Wolfe ascend the steps into the house, shaking her head and carrying the train of her dress skirt so she wouldn't trip.

Stephanie rolled her eyes so that only Dad and Madison could see.

"Stephanie . . ." Dad said in a low voice. Madison knew that voice. It was the way Dad sounded when he was stressed out.

"Don't say it. Please," Stephanie replied.

"We said this would be a small wedding, right?" Dad asked. "Well, I see about a hundred or more people here already for the rehearsal. What is that? I think I have been patient and tolerant and . . ."

"Jeff!" Stephanie said, turning her head toward Madison. "Maddie is right here. Can't we talk about this when we have a moment alone?"

Madison tried to look away, but she heard everything.

"A moment alone?" Dad exclaimed. "Now, that's a joke."

Stephanie tugged Dad's sleeve and pulled him out of earshot of the other guests, although Madison could still hear him loud and clear.

"We need to discuss this *privately*," Stephanie said again.

Dad looked as though steam might blow out of his ears at any moment. His cheeks were getting red.

"There's nothing to discuss," he said. "This is not what I wanted. I didn't think it was what you wanted, either. And yet, here we are. I brought Madison here all the way from New York. She's miserable and uncomfortable. I'm not feeling all that great, either. . . ."

Stephanie looked away as though she were on the verge of tears again.

"Please don't do this, Jeff. Not now. Not right before everything starts."

"Well, why don't you tell me when it would be a good time?" Dad asked.

"This is my home," Stephanie said. "Can't we please get through the next day here? That's all I ask."

Dad shook his head. "We'll talk later," he said abruptly, and marched up the stairs without Stephanie and without Madison.

Stephanie headed up the stairs alone.

Madison stared straight ahead, not saying a word.

"Hey!" a voice chirped at Madison from somewhere behind her. It was Kirk.

"Hey," she mumbled.

"Where's your dad and Aunt Steph?" Kirk asked.

Madison shrugged. "Inside somewhere. They just walked in."

"Want to go raid the hors d'oeuvres table over there?" Kirk asked. "There's good stuff on it. Are you hungry?"

Madison shook her head. "Not really. But I'll go with you."

So they walked inside *together*. Although Madison was still distressed about not entering the party with Dad, she felt better walking inside with someone as cute as Kirk.

In addition to pots of budding Texas wildflowers, the entryway was bursting with music. The Wolfes had hired a local mariachi band to play for the rehearsal event. While guests entertained themselves with good food and good music, participating family members could sneak away for a run-through of the ceremony.

Madison was reminded of Drew's parents' theme parties. In fact, Drew's mom and Stephanie's mom had a lot in common. Mrs. Maxwell and Mrs. Wolfe both circulated at their own parties like queen bees. And Madison felt just as out of place here as she did sometimes at Drew's house.

How was a person supposed to act at a fancy barbecue?

Standing off to the side of one ballroom, Madison spotted Tiffany and some of the other cousins. Just as Madison had expected, Tiffany was dressed up like a Barbie doll, with every hair in place and every color matching. Madison looked down at her own peasant skirt and shirt. She felt under-dressed and over-wrinkled.

"Kirk!" Tiffany called out, excluding Madison from her hello.

"Tiff!" Kirk said.

Madison smiled in Tiffany's direction. "You look nice tonight, Tiffany."

"Gee, thanks a bunch!" Tiffany said, fluffing up a handful of her blond curls. She didn't say a word about Madison's outfit. She was too busy scanning the room.

"Let's hit the food," Kirk said with a grunt.

Madison laughed. He was like a dream boy, hav-ing all the best qualities of all her good guy friends. Right now, Kirk reminded Madison of Egg—or maybe Dan, the pig-out king.

"I'm not really hungry," Tiffany said, pursing her lips.

"What are you—a person or a stick? You never eat," Kirk snapped. "Well, Madison and I are making our move."

Madison held in her giggles as she followed Kirk toward the long food tables.

"I feel like all anyone does around here is eat," Madison said.

Kirk shoved a hunk of cheese and a cracker into his mouth. "Hmmmf?" he asked, chewing.

Madison chuckled and casually looked around the room to see if she could find Dad anywhere. She wanted to see if he was feeling better, or at least feeling a little less angry.

But he wasn't in the room where they were standing.

A plate of mini–corn dogs distracted Kirk, so Madison wandered out onto a side patio. It had a full view of the property. On a side lawn she could see Stephanie and Mrs. Wolfe. Although Madison couldn't make out what they were saying, she knew it was some kind of argument. Stephanie kept shaking her head and waving her arms in the air, while her mother motionless, her arms crossed in front of her.

Across the yard on the other side, Madison finally spotted Dad, standing by an old tree. He gazed off into the distance. A group of cattle stood flapping their tails at flies and nibbling at the grass. Near the cattle was a small lake. Madison knew it was Bobcat Lake, where the ceremony would be taking place the very next day.

At the same time, Madison saw Stephanie turn away from her mother and march across to where Dad was standing.

It was like watching a movie in slow motion.

"There you are!"

Madison whirled around to see Kirk at the doorway to the patio.

"Everyone's looking for you," Kirk said. "They want to start the wedding rehearsal. Aunt Steph and your dad and everyone are hanging near the lake. Come on!"

"Oh!" Madison said. She followed Kirk back in to the main part of the house, clutching her flowered purse close by her side. Madison unhooked the latch of the purse and pulled out the book of love poems. Then she followed Kirk back outside.

Dad's eyes lit up when he saw Madison walk outside. He threw his arm around her shoulder and whispered in her ear.

"I don't mean to wander off like that," Dad explained. "I was just a little steamed."

Madison shrugged. "I know, Dad. So, what am I supposed to do next?"

Dad bowed his head. "Here comes the boss," he whispered. "Let's ask her."

Mrs. Wolfe came over and clapped her hands to get everyone's attention.

"We want to start! Let's all get together here, shall we?" Mrs. Wolfe said.

Stephanie stood, tight-lipped, behind her mother. The other members of the wedding party formed a tight cluster in front of a makeshift altar that had been set up near the edge of the lake. On the side, there was an old wooden gazebo decorated with winding green ivy and paper streamers.

Madison wondered if anyone else there sensed the tension between Dad and Stephanie and Stephanie's mom. It seemed that no one noticed

184

anything. People babbled about the hors d'oeuvres and the setting, not the wedding couple. As far as most family members and guests were concerned, Dad and Stephanie were the picture of perfection.

But Madison knew better. Something was up.

"Now, you stand over here. . . ." Mrs. Wolfe began directing people as to where they should stand, but the pastor performing the ceremony soon interrupted her. He strolled up wearing his black garments and carrying a leather-bound Bible. Madison noticed that he didn't stop smiling.

"Di-yaaan," Pastor John drawled. "I think we can do just fine if y'all let *me* tell these fine people where to stand. Sound good?"

Mrs. Wolfe giggled a little, embarrassed. "Take it away, Pastor John. Of course! Of course!"

Stephanie's father took his wife by the elbow and gently walked her to the side of the crowd.

Members of the wedding party talked nonstop. It was hard for Pastor John to be heard over the din of the crowd. He asked the girls to stand on the right, and boys, the left.

The four bridesmaids (Tiffany, her cousins Rebecca and Lynne, and Stephanie's sister Bethany) stood in an arc around the junior maid of honor Madison—and the maid of honor, Wanda. Stephanie was in the center.

"This is sooooo pretty," Tiffany gushed. "Aunt

Steph, this is soooo exciting and you look soooo gorgeous. . . ."

Tiffany continued with her incessant chatter. *Why wasn't anyone telling her to shut up?* Madison wanted to thump Miss Texas Poison Ivy on the back and say, "Um . . . clue phone, it's for you! You're not supposed to be talking now! Hello?"

But she didn't do or say anything. Right now, Madison was too preoccupied with thoughts of the Shakespearean sonnet she had to recite in just a few minutes, in front of everyone. . . .

Madison's knees were shaking.

Across the makeshift aisle, Stephanie's father, Mr. Wolfe, stood in as Dad's best man, since Uncle Rick had not yet arrived. Kirk was the junior best man—*and* Madison's counterpart for the ceremony.

Kirk kept flashing one smile after another. Madison hoped he was smiling at her, but she couldn't be sure.

Stephanie fussed with the hem of her skirt.

Dad tried to calm her down.

And Tiffany kept talking, talking, talking. . . .

What was going on? This was unlike any wedding Madison had ever imagined. She wanted to scream.

Instead, she focused on the water in the lake. It looked beautiful on the surface but muddy underneath—a little like her whole experience of Texas so far. Since Madison had arrived in Bellville, everything had seemed festive and happy, but underneath that surface, tongues had been wagging and stress building.

Madison realized something else, too, as she stared out at the lake and watched everyone fussing and fighting before the run-through began. Although the groomsmen were standing up for Dad, they weren't his real family. Not the way she was.

In truth, Madison was the only *real* representative of the Finn family at Bobcat Lake until the next day, when Uncle Rick and Aunt Violet were due to arrive. It was as if Stephanie's family had taken over everything having to do with the wedding; Madison felt them closing in around her and Dad like the tentacles of an octopus.

The big squeeze.

Madison closed her eyes and tried to think it all away.

Chapter 14

Eventually, the wedding crowd settled down.

A cool breeze blew in off the lake and everyone paid close attention to Father John's words.

The official ceremony run-through began.

It seemed as if it were getting off to a good start. Madison was even breathing normally.

But then Mrs. Wolfe again started to direct the wedding party, like an orchestra conductor. Madison smelled trouble as she watched Mrs. Wolfe point and mumble, waving her arm like a conductor's baton.

Two flower girls and the ring bearer wandered up an "aisle," and pretended to drop rose petals from teeny baskets.

One of the little girls dropped her basket and fell down. She started to cry.

"Shhhhhh!" Mrs. Wolfe growled at the little girl, helping to lift her back up off the ground. She gently guided her back into the arms of her mother, a college friend of Stephanie's, who stood on the sidelines.

Stephanie turned to her mother. "I don't think we're going to need rose petals," she said quietly. "Let's just have the girls follow me. That way they don't have to—"

"Nonsense!" Mrs. Wolfe said, rolling her eyes. "Of course we need rose petals," she insisted. "This whole ceremony has been carefully constructed."

Dad looked steamed. But he kept his mouth shut.

Pastor John invited any members of the wedding party who still had not done so to take their positions. Madison faced Kirk. She couldn't take her eyes off him. Madison had decided Kirk would be her distraction from everything else.

What would Kirk look like in a tuxedo? Madison wondered. *Definitely* cuter than Hart, she decided, even though she was pretty sure no one could ever really take the place of her crush from home.

Stephanie's father performed the first reading of the ceremony. He read a passage from the Bible, skipping certain parts when Pastor John gave him some secret signal. Time was running out, and they still needed to get through more than three-quarters of the rehearsal.

The breeze from the lake died down. Madison could see everyone beginning to perspire again. By now, Stephanie and Dad weren't really looking at each other. Everyone seemed a little distracted.

When Pastor John announced, "Now we get to the second reading," Madison stood at full attention. She fumbled for the book of poems and made her way to the same spot where Stephanie's father had stood. In the midst of all this, she would prove what a good daughter she was. Madison Francesca Finn would give the best wedding reading of all time.

"A sonnet," Madison began, her voice shaking a little.

Steady, steady . . .

"Hold it!" Mrs. Wolfe shouted, jumping up from her chair.

Madison dropped the green leather book on the ground.

"Oh, Mother! What is it now?" Stephanie asked.

"Just a little something . . ." Mrs. Wolfe said.

Dad gritted his teeth. "I think we need to keep this rehearsal moving along. . . ."

"Jeffrey," Diane replied. "This is important! The position of the altar is all wrong. The view down to the lake isn't quite right. Now you don't want something like that to mess up the whole ceremony, do you?"

"Mess up what? I think the position is fine," Dad barked.

"Mother, sit down," Stephanie groaned.

"Yes, sit down, Diane," Dad said.

"I think I can handle this, Jeff," Stephanie said to Dad, holding him back with one hand. "Mother, *sit*."

"Stephanie Mae, I only want the very best for you both," Mrs. Wolfe said. "There is no need to get angry with me."

Madison bent over to pick up her fallen book. Out of the corner of her eye, she saw Tiffany and the other girls giggling.

Were they laughing at Madison?

Kirk leaned over to Madison. "What's up with *them*?" he asked. At first Madison thought he was speaking about Tiffany and the girls, but then she realized he was referring to Stephanie, Dad, and Mrs. Wolfe.

Now *everyone* had to sense—and see—the tension.

"Look, Diane," Dad said, pushing himself closer to Stephanie's mother. "We've all had a wonderful time at these parties and events. You've outdone yourself, and I am forever in your debt. But right now, I'd like the ceremony to be what Stephanie and I want. I think the view is fine. Stephanie thinks it's fine. Okay?"

Madison gulped. She imagined giant claws popping out of Mrs. Wolfe's fingers.

Attack of the Mother-in-Law-to-Be.

"Mother, please understand. . . ." Stephanie said, trying to soften the blow.

Mrs. Wolfe flared her nostrils like a caged animal and let out a little sigh. "I don't understand. I was only trying to help. Is this the thanks I get?"

"Please, Diane," Dad continued, easing his tone a little. "You *are* helpful, but can you let us do this one thing on our own?"

Stephanie looked ready to explode into screams or tears or both.

Madison raised her hand to ask a question, as if she were back in school. "Um . . . should I finish the reading?" she asked aloud.

Pastor John placed his hand on Madison's shoulder. "Now doesn't seem to be a good time. I'm sure you'll do a lovely job tomorrow," he whispered to her. "Let's see if your parents can resolve these other issues first."

Madison backed away, nearly toppling into Kirk.

"This is wiggy," Kirk whispered.

"Wiggier than wiggy," Madison said.

She wanted to run.

No.

She wanted to *grab Dad* and then run.

The other people present at the rehearsal seemed to get the hint, finally, that things were getting a little off track. People began to disperse, heading back in for more hors d'oeuvres or drinks, or heading to the driveway to retrieve their cars and make their way to the rehearsal dinner site.

Dad did his best to try calming Stephanie, but she only blubbered all the more, shooing his advances away with a frantic wave of her hand.

Then someone told the mariachi band to start playing again, which only added to the confusion.

"I think we all have the right idea," Pastor John said gently. "We just need a little direction now."

He pulled Stephanie and Dad off to the side to speak with them privately.

At the same time, Stephanie's father tugged Mrs. Wolfe away in the opposite direction.

"This isn't what weddings are supposed to be like," Madison said to Kirk. "Where is everyone going?"

Kirk just shrugged. "Hey, at least the food is good."

"The food?" Madison said. *Was he kidding?*

Tiffany came over. "What is up with your dad?" she asked Madison.

"What are you talking about? It isn't *all* my dad's fault," Madison said with a hint of anger.

"Well, he isn't being very nice to my grandmother," Tiffany said.

Madison looked away, wishing Aimee and Fiona were nearby so she could have them on her side.

"Your grandmother isn't being very nice, either," Madison said.

"Whoa! Whoa!" Kirk interrupted. "What are we supposed to do now? Is everyone going to dinner or what? I'm hungry."

"Hungry?" Madison asked.

"What?" Kirk asked.

Madison couldn't help cracking a smile.

Tiffany made a pig noise, and Kirk's eyes flashed.

"Quit it, Tiff!" he snapped.

Kirk grabbed his cousin and messed up her hair. Tiffany let out a shriek.

"You are such dead meat!" she wailed.

Madison was sure Tiffany would break into tears. Her perfect 'do was done for. She gave Kirk a push.

Tiffany's mother, Wanda, came over toward the kids. "Hey y'all, let's take it easy over here. I think the rehearsal is over now," she said.

"*Over?* Like, totally over?" Madison asked.

She thought they would just take a break while Dad, Stephanie, and Mrs. Wolfe cooled off.

She looked around to see if Dad or Stephanie had wandered back from their chat with Pastor John. But they were nowhere to be seen.

"We're going to head over to the restaurant now. Do you want to come in the minivan with us, Madison?" Wanda asked.

"I think I'll go ride with Aunt Bethany instead," Tiffany piped up.

"What are you talking 'bout?" Wanda clucked

194

her tongue. "We're riding together. Madison, are you with us?"

Tiffany rolled her eyes.

"Um . . . that's really nice of you. . . ." Madison started to say. "But . . . um . . ."

Madison didn't want to go off in their car. She didn't want to be squashed in the backseat with the Texas twin of her enemy. Madison wanted to ride with Dad, not them.

Where was Dad?

"Well, hon," Wanda said, looking around. "We may be your only ride. I think your dad and Stephanie are going in one of the limousines."

"Oh," Madison said. "Um . . . would you excuse me for a sec?"

Madison turned away from Wanda, Tiffany, and the others and dashed into a bathroom located in the small, blue cabin alongside the lake. She splashed a little water on her face and primped in front of the mirror, trying to get a strand of hair to stay in place that kept flying out of its clip. But the hard, fluorescent light inside the bathroom didn't help Madison feel any better. It only shone a glow on her sweatier-than-sweaty forehead. A small blemish had just started to pop out along the side of her nose.

Madison reached for a tissue and blew her nose hard, hoping that somehow her pimple would magically disappear. . . .

And that somehow Dad would magically reappear.

Instead, she heard a knock on the bathroom door.

"Are y'all coming or what?" Tiffany said.

Three different parties located in three different, huge ballrooms packed the Great Hall restaurant to overflowing. People lined the halls waiting for service at the bars. Madison, Tiffany, and Kirk walked into the room designated for the Wolfe and Finn wedding. The other cousins were already inside.

"I don't see your dad or Aunt Stephanie anywhere," Tiffany remarked.

Madison kept looking. "They have to be here," she said, still desperate to make her getaway.

Wanda put her arm around Madison. "Are you feeling alrighty, hon?" Wanda asked. "I know this is a big day, and things are a little crazy right now. . . ."

Madison looked up at Wanda. "Huh?" she said. She didn't feel like having a heart-to-heart right now, especially with yet another person from Stephanie's family. "Oh, I'm fine," she said softly, trying hard to be nice.

Deep down, Madison felt a pang like the kind she had used to get when she slept over at someone's house.

There was a word for that feeling.

Homesick.

She envisioned Phinnie, sniffing around his chair and pillows. What Madison wouldn't give to have just one doggy kiss from him right now! She closed her eyes for a split second—as if doing that would somehow send a secret psychic message to Mom.

Where was Dad?

"Hey, look at the food spread," Kirk said, appearing with his arms outstretched.

He was a welcome sight, coming over and tugging on Madison's sleeve.

"You have to see this. Grandma has, like, twenty ice sculptures here," Kirk continued. "Roses, a spur, and a lasso . . ."

"*More* food?" Madison cried. She followed Kirk inside to see the ice figures.

Tiffany came up behind them. "Boo!" she said.

Madison was about to turn around and scare Tiffany right back, but then she saw Dad across the room. He was standing very close to Stephanie.

"Hey, look," Tiffany said, as soon as she'd spotted them, too. "Aunt Steph and your dad are holding hands again. That's a good thing."

Madison nodded. "Yeah," she said blankly.

Tiffany looked at Madison, crossing her eyes. "Well, duh!" she said in a bright, twangy voice. "'Course it's good. They're getting hitched tomorrow. At least, I think that's why we're all here. I knew they'd make up after fighting."

Madison turned away to see Mrs. Wolfe on the

other side of the room. She looked as chipper as ever.

"Maddie!" Dad called out across the room. "You're here!"

Madison immediately ditched Tiffany and bounded across the room toward Dad. He gave her a hug.

"I'm sorry I didn't see you before we left the run-through," he said.

Madison sighed. "I forgive you, Dad. I'm just glad you're here now. . . ."

"How are you holding up?" Dad asked.

"Fine . . ." Madison said. "How are *you* holding up?"

"Um . . . Stephanie and I are fine, too," Dad said calmly. "I think. For now."

Madison hated how her dad was answering for both himself and Stephanie. That was how Dad would see things from now on, she thought.

"What happened back at the ranch?" Madison asked.

"You got me," Dad said with a shrug. "Diane tries so hard sometimes, but, with the rush of plans and all that—I think she got a little carried away."

"You sounded so angry," Madison said. "I've never heard you talk like that."

Dad laughed. "Nonsense!" he said. "Sure, you have. I get mad a lot."

Madison giggled. "No, you do not."

Dad threw his arms into the air. "No? Well . . . I'm going to have to start getting madder, aren't I?"

"Please don't," Madison said, giving Dad another hug. She wished that holding him tight in a hug could keep Dad from changing altogether.

The rehearsal dinner got under way a lot faster than the run-through at Bobcat Lake had. After a round of "three cheers for the bride and groom" toasts, Dad and Stephanie made their own little speeches, thanking the guests for coming to their special party. Dad added a little piece to his toast that referred directly to Madison.

"As you can see, I'm a little outnumbered in the guest department," Dad said, with his glass raised to the ceiling. "But my daughter, Maddie, makes up for all of it. She's here watching over me."

Stephanie was the first person to clap, and then the whole room broke into a wave of applause.

Tiffany leaned over and whispered in Madison's ear. "You must be so embarrassed," she said, not really clapping.

Madison made a face. Embarrassed? She wasn't embarrassed at all.

Instead, Madison was feeling surprisingly choked up by the turn of events. Only a few hours earlier, she'd been feeling sick about the wedding.

What did Tiffany know?

After the rehearsal dinner there was a little more dancing, but the dance floor was small, and hardly anyone seemed interested. The most energetic people on the dance floor were Dad and Stephanie, who were back to being their lovey-dovey selves again.

It wasn't until the end of the evening that Dad wandered over toward Madison with his arms wide open.

"Okay, honey bear! It's your turn!" he said. "Will you dance with me?"

Madison looked over her shoulder, pretending that he was talking to someone else. "Um . . . no way, Dad!"

Dad grabbed her anyway. "One dance," he said. "And then we'll head back to the hotel, okay?"

Madison glanced around to see who was watching. She didn't see Tiffany or Kirk anywhere. She could feel her knees buckling.

"Dad," she said softly. "I really don't want to. . . ."

But Dad grabbed both of Madison's wrists and pulled her along with him.

As they spun across the dance floor, Dad squeezed Madison close, hugging her and dancing with her at the same time. Surprisingly, all of Madison's Texas anxiety fell away like a heavy cloak.

Now, Madison felt a little more like a princess, swirling around on the dance floor in her peasant skirt, hugging her dad tight. Madison closed her eyes and felt the music lift her up and down and around. . . .

Her imagination took over.

What would it be like to dance with a boyfriend she loved—who maybe loved her, too?

Was this what it would be like if Hart Jones held her in *his* arms?

Did love always feel like floating?

Dad twirled Madison until she was really and truly dizzy. Ceiling and wall decorations blended together in a blur of stars and glitter. She grabbed Dad's arm to steady her balance. Together they applauded the band when the song ended. That was when Stephanie came over. She was clapping, too.

"You two looked perfect out there!" Stephanie gushed. "What a pair."

Madison felt that maybe Stephanie was saying nice things just to butter her up. After all, the moment of truth had arrived. The wedding was tomorrow. Stephanie needed to step quickly into the role of supportive, encouraging stepmother, didn't she?

"I think everyone's heading home," Stephanie whispered to Dad. "Are you two heading back to the hotel?"

Dad nodded. He reached out for Madison's hand, and she gave it to him.

"Well, I'm heading back to the ranch, then," Stephanie said with a little gasp, as if she'd finally let it sink in that she was getting married the following day. "See you tomorrow. . . ."

Stephanie started to giggle.

Dad did, too.

Madison stood back, watching the two of them say their last good-night as singles. Of course, she had to turn away when they kissed. Madison dreamed of kissing boys more than she dreamed of almost anything else. But right now, the sight of her dad locking lips with Stephanie made her a little queasy.

After Dad and Stephanie finally parted for good, waving and blowing more kisses, Dad wandered over to a few of the other guests and shook their hands. Madison sat down at a table alone, picking at a snag on the tablecloth. The blue, digital clock on the wall said 10:11.

A moment later, Dad came over and knelt in front of Madison. "What are you doing all the way over here?" he asked.

"I'm waiting for you. Can we go now?" Madison asked. "You told Stephanie we were leaving. So why are we still here?"

"Hold on!" Dad said. He stood up again and held up a single finger, as if to say *Just one more minute.*

Madison slumped back in her chair.

Who was Dad going to talk to now?

Madison didn't feel like saying good night to anyone else—especially not Tiffany.

Fifteen minutes later, when Dad finally returned to collect Madison and head for the door, Madison's mood lifted.

They walked out of the restaurant into the hot Texas night air.

A taxicab was there, waiting to take them back to the hotel.

Chapter 15

The ride back to the Bellville Villas was surprisingly quiet, as if Madison and Dad had run out of things to say.

The only real sounds were the sound of Dad humming to himself (it sounded like one of the love songs that had been playing at the rehearsal), and the low drone of crickets and other insects outside.

Madison spied the Texas moon through the window of the car and made a quick wish.

Please don't let this wedding happen.

No sooner had she thought the words, however, than Madison wanted to take them back. How could she wish for something so . . . *unkind*?

All the same, Madison had real reasons for

wanting to see the wedding called off. She would have to recount them in a file as soon as she had a chance.

1. Mrs. Wolfe wasn't playing fair, and Madison didn't want a step-grandmother like that. Besides, what did Madison want with a new cousin like Tiffany?

2. Mega-omens were all around. Madison was worried. Was Dad's union with Stephanie doomed? It sure felt like it. Madison had spent the last year saddened by the Big D. She wasn't sure she could deal with the Big D–2.

3. Somewhere inside, in a teeny little corner of her heart, Madison still secretly wanted Mom and Dad to get back together. Was it so wrong to hope, even though she knew Mom and Dad could not get along, and even though she knew they had tried to get back together and failed?

Dad kept up his humming as they got out of the taxi, rode upstairs in the elevator, and walked down the corridor to the hotel rooms.

Madison pushed her card key into the door first.

"I'll come in with you," Dad said, following her inside.

"Oh," Madison said. "You will?"

Dad let out a huge breath as soon as they'd walked inside. "I can't believe I'm getting married tomorrow, can you?" he asked.

"Nope," Madison said, collapsing onto the bed.

"What a whirlwind," Dad said, wiping his brow. He smiled. "Stephanie and I were talking tonight about how great it's going to be once we get back to Far Hills."

"Great," Madison said under her breath.

"Don't you think it will be great?" Dad asked. He eyed Madison up and down. "What's with the sourpuss?"

"Nothing," Madison grumbled.

Dad shrugged his shoulders and gave her a kiss on the forehead. "Well, off to bed. I need my beauty sleep," Dad joked.

Madison didn't laugh. She clicked on the T.V. instead.

"First, I'm going to check and see if Uncle Rick and Aunt Violet or any of my other friends have checked in yet, okay?" Dad said.

Madison nodded without really looking at Dad.

"See you bright and early?" Dad asked.

Madison nodded. "Uh-huh," she said, changing the channel.

As soon as Dad had gone out, Madison turned off the T.V. set and pulled out her laptop.

She didn't need the tube. She needed a serious BFF fix.

Her e-mailbox blinked with a few messages—all of them from friends.

```
FROM                    SUBJECT
✉ Bigwheels             I almost forgot!!!
✉ Balletgrl             Fiona
✉ Sk8rboy               Summer BBQ Sat.
```

Bigwheels had written again. That was twice in one day!

Madison clicked on the e-mail.

```
From: Bigwheels
To: MadFinn
Subject: I almost forgot!!!
Date: Fri 19 July 4:03 PM
```
How are u? I know I just wrote this
morning but I had 2 write again. I
forgot 2 ask u to e-mail me n e
photos from the wedding so I
can see ur dress. I bet ur the
prettiest girl there. That's like
something my mom would say. But I
bet it's true.

Hang in there.

Yours till the polka dots,

Bigwheels aka Vicki

Madison hit SAVE **so she could write back to Bigwheels later.**

Next, she found a message from Aimee.

From: Balletgrl
To: MadFinn
Subject: Fiona
Date: Fri 19 July 6:55 PM
_____

Im writing b/c I know u would want
to know that things here are pretty
bad. I guess Fiona's Dad had some
kind of relapse and he's back in
serious or critical condition. I
feel so helpless. Fiona cries all
the time now. What am I supposed to
do? I wish u were here so we BOTH
could make her feel bettr. U have 2
hurry home!!

My mom says Mrs. Waters is not
doing too well either which is a
major bummer. I think my mom and
your mom and Senora Diaz are all
going over to Fiona's house to help
her deal with what's happening. I'll
e-mail u more details 18r.

I miss you so much, Maddie. Fiona
isn't the same since all this
happened and Far Hills feels so
weird without you being here. I

have a super long dance class
tomorrow so I might not e-mail
right back, but e me anyhow,
please? Promise?

Love, Aim

Madison had to keep that promise in mind. It
seemed more important than anything else just
then. She couldn't believe that she was sitting in the
middle of Texas while her friends were going
through such a rough time.

This wasn't where she belonged. Was it?

Finally, Madison opened the last and final e-mail.
She almost dropped her laptop when she read the
"From" line.

It was from none other than Hart Jones.

```
From: Sk8ingBoy
To: DantheMan; TheEggMan; W_Wonka7;
Peace-peep; L8RG8R; Wetwinz;
Wetwins; Balletgrl; MadFinn;
Rokstarr; 0712biggy; DougLee;
B_Foster; SkatrGod; Kickit88;
CharlieX; JK4Ever; RosyROSE;
Flowr99; LuvNstuff
Re: Summer BBQ Sat.
Date: Fri July 8:21 PM
```

Okay guys here's the deal the BBQ
is now starting l8r so don't show
up until after 12 ok? Thanx

p.s. we will be playing VB girls
vs. boys, see ya

Madison's stomach churned.

Fiona needed her.

Aimee missed her.

And Hart was having a barbecue?

Why wasn't she in Far Hills *right now*?

"Wait a sec!" Dad said, walking back into Madison's room. She nearly jumped out of her skin when she saw him come through the divider door.

There was no time to think about Fiona *or* Hart. Dad had one of those serious, "don't mess with me" looks on his face.

Madison closed her laptop. "What's up, Dad?" she asked.

"I should ask you the same thing," Dad said.

Madison looked at Dad like he had three heads. "Huh?"

Dad nodded. "You hardly spoke all the way home."

"Oh, Dad," Madison sighed. "I'm fine."

Dad leaned in close. "Maddie," he whispered. "What's wrong?"

Madison felt her stomach flip-flop. Maybe it was the words Dad was saying, or maybe it was the way he was saying them. She wasn't sure. But those two words put her stomach in knots.

"Tomorrow," Madison said simply, in response.

Dad closed his eyes. "You're still not comfortable with the idea of me getting married, are you?"

"I can't talk to you anymore about this. . . ." Madison said. "It's not like it would make a difference, anyhow."

"Now what is *that* supposed to mean?" Dad asked.

"Nothing," Madison grumbled. She lay back on the pillows and bit her lip. There was no way she was going to talk about that anymore. She wanted to get back to her e-mails from Aimee and Hart and everyone else.

"Look, Maddie," Dad said. "I know this has been an insane trip. First your luggage got lost. Then we had trouble at the dinner the first night—and at all the parties. I wish I could do some things differently, believe me. . . ."

"I miss home. I miss my friends," Madison said.

"But you'll see them in a day or so," Dad said. Then he paused. "Oh. Are you talking about Fiona—and what happened with her dad?"

Madison looked away. "Maybe. Whatever."

"Honey," Dad said. "I know you want to be there for her. And you will be. Even though it's hard, I really need you to be here for me, too."

Madison closed her eyes. "I'm trying, Dad. . . ."

"I can imagine how you feel, Maddie. You feel bad about Fiona. And, as far as the wedding goes, we've tried to make the plans work for you, but maybe that was just wishful thinking. . . ." Dad said.

Madison rolled away from Dad.

"I don't want you to be angry like this," Dad said.

Madison sighed again.

"You have to talk to me more," Dad pleaded.

But Madison wouldn't talk. She wouldn't cry. She held her breath and made her second huge wish of the evening.

Please make Dad just go away.

"Okay. I'm not leaving this bedroom until you talk to me," Dad said.

He reached around and pulled Madison toward him. Madison found herself staring right into his big eyes.

"I don't have anything to s—s—say. . . ." Madison stammered, trying to look away so she wouldn't get upset.

Dad sat down on the bed next to Madison. Their heads were side by side. It got very quiet in the hotel room.

"I wish I could explain to you how I feel right now. I've tried telling you before about me and Stephanie, but I am not sure you really have understood."

"I know, I know," Madison said. "I'm not a dummy, Dad."

"I don't think you're a dummy, sweetheart. I just think that you need to look beyond the surface of things sometimes."

Madison thought again about Bobcat Lake. She *did* see. Beyond the surface was muddier than muddy.

"Dad, can we talk about something else?" Madison asked.

"What else is there to talk about right now, Maddie?" Dad asked. He stared up at the ceiling.

"What are you thinking about now?" Madison asked, after a few more moments of silence.

"In ten hours, I will marry Stephanie, and more than anything else on this planet, I want *you* to be okay with it," Dad said.

"I told you a zillion times, Dad, I'm okay with it," Madison lied.

"I believed you before," Dad said. "I'm not so sure anymore."

Madison sat up on the bed. "Why don't you believe me now?" she asked. "I can't believe you don't believe that I believe . . ."

Dad made a face. "What?"

"Oh, forget it!" Madison said, frustrated by her inability to articulate what was on her mind. "You know what I mean!"

"I believe that you want the best for me, Maddie. . . ." Dad's voice trailed off. He looked into her eyes. "Are you scared you might lose me?"

Madison gulped. She wasn't willing to admit that. No way.

"What are you talking about?" Madison asked.

Dad nodded. "You know."

"Are you *really* marrying Stephanie tomorrow?" Madison asked, as if *not* marrying Stephanie were an option Dad was considering.

"Of course I am," Dad said, without hesitation.

"But her family is so weird," Madison said. "And she's so . . . neurotic. She practically bawled her eyes out that night in here with me. Definitely not a good sign, Dad. You need someone else. Someone better."

"Oh, Maddie," Dad said thoughtfully.

"I don't get it, Dad," Madison said.

"Love doesn't always make sense, honey bear. You'll find love yourself someday. Then you will know what I'm talking about."

Pictures of Drew . . . and Kirk . . . and then *Hart* flashed through Madison's mind.

Dad sounded like a Hallmark greeting card. But he was making some sense.

Someday she would find love.

"It's getting late," Dad said, finally lifting himself off the bed. "And *I'm getting married in the morning.*" He was singing the tune from *My Fair Lady*.

"That's it? You're going?" Madison said, grabbing for his leg as she had done when she was little.

Dad gently grabbed her hands and pulled them away.

"Is Uncle Rick here yet?" Madison asked.

Dad nodded. "They'll see us in the morning," Dad said. "Why don't you try to get some sleep now?"

"Right," Madison said. "You have a big day tomorrow."

"Correction," Dad said. "*We* have a big day tomorrow."

"Okay, *we*," Madison said. She threw her arms around his waist. "We have a big day tomorrow. We. We. We."

Dad turned and headed back into the adjoining room with a wink and a blown kiss. "You just sleep tight, Maddie," he said as he pulled the door shut.

As soon as he had vanished from sight, Madison's chest heaved. If her life had ever bordered on soap opera, Madison thought, it was doing so now.

Whom could she talk to?

She wished that Bigwheels were online so they could chat.

She wished that Fiona weren't in the middle of her dad crisis or that Aimee weren't sleeping, so that they could all chat.

There was only one person left who could lift Madison's spirits now.

She picked up the phone and dialed Mom.

"Hello?" a groggy voice answered on the other end. Madison realized that back in Far Hills it was way after one o'clock in the morning.

"Mom?" she said.

"Maddie?" Mom said. "Is that you?"

"I forgot how late it was," Madison said. "Sorry."

"Oh," Mom said, trying to snap out of her sleepiness. "Is something wrong, Maddie?" she asked.

"No," Madison said quickly. "I just . . ."

"You sound funny."

"Yes . . . I mean, no," Madison said. "I'm fine."

"Oh," Mom said. "So you just called to wake me up, then?"

"I guess. You better go back to sleep. I'm really, really sorry."

"Maddie?" Mom said. "Why don't you call me in the morning, when my eyes aren't glued together and I can actually talk like a normal person?"

"Dad's getting married tomorrow."

"I know," Mom said sweetly. She paused. "Are you sure you're okay, honey bear?"

"Yes, yes," Madison said. "Well, I think so."

"And you're sure you can wait to talk until morning?" Mom asked.

"Yeah," Madison said. "Give Phin a kiss for me. I love you guys!"

"We love you, too," Mom said. "Sleep tight."

Madison was still saying the words "I love you" when Mom hung up the phone. Madison hung up on her end, too, and rolled back onto the bed. Her stomach felt as if she'd just ridden on the loopiest roller coaster in the world.

Was it because of all the things Dad had said about Stephanie?

Was it all that talk about love?

Love.

Madison had totally lied to Dad. Of course she knew about love. After all, that was really the only thing that explained how she felt about Hart Jones.

Love.

It was a big, pink thing that made her head spin.

And with what little she knew about love, Madison began to understand why tomorrow's wedding day must go on—no matter what.

Chapter 16

Around three in the morning, Madison opened her eyes in a panic.

The hotel room was totally dark except for a pale white glow around the curtains, where a little light seeped in from the parking lot and the city of Bellville.

The collage!

She sat up in bed and clicked on the side-table light.

With all the parties and rehearsals and heart-to-heart chats with Dad, Madison had forgotten to finish pulling together all the pieces of her wedding collage for Dad and Stephanie.

And she was supposed to be giving it to them as a gift in just a few hours!

Madison threw off the blankets and jumped out of bed. She reached underneath the bed to find her stash of collage materials.

She laid out the pages of the collage that she had already finished. A few pages needed some more borders of foil and stickers and glued-down words. Madison scrambled for her materials. She couldn't believe that she'd been working on it for only a few days now and here she was, putting on the finishing touches in the middle of the night.

Madison yawned.

She wasn't even sure she would be able to stay awake and finish the whole thing. And the television wasn't much help in keeping her awake. There was nothing interesting on—just some infomercials about skin care and chicken roasters. And the more she thought about Fiona and her dad and how much she missed Far Hills . . .

She had to keep her mind on the collage! By the light of the hotel lamp, Madison turned her full attention to the last touches of gluing and snipping. Somehow, with the help of some woven ribbon, she pulled everything together, so that the only thing left was to write the poem.

The poem.

Madison had tried out several different—and unsuccessful—versions of the poem during the week. It was going to take some more deep thinking, and unfortunately, Madison was sure that all of her brain cells were on *snooze* at that moment.

She yawned again. And then finished the poem.

The clock said five-thirty. A yellow light crept across the carpet. Morning was on its way.

Madison wished that Phinnie were there in the room with her. He'd know the right thing to say, in doggy talk. He'd nuzzle her feet with his wet nose. Phin always knew what it took to make Madison happy, before, during, and after a stress-out period.

But Phin wasn't there. She had to do this all on her own.

Madison peeked into the closet and pulled out her long, orange, tie-dyed dress. It sparkled in the dim light. For a split second, Madison wondered if maybe the dress would clash with the wedding cake or the hoedown favors, but then she stopped worrying.

No matter what the circumstances, Madison was going to be herself—orange dress, orange shoes, and all the rest.

Besides, she'd already accepted the fact that Tiffany and the other cousins would be more dressed up than she was.

Beeeeeeeeeeeeeeep.

A very loud beep echoed in the room, and Madison shot a look at the alarm clock. She had pre-set it so she wouldn't oversleep.

Now all she could do was laugh.

Oversleep? Ha!

It was close to six-thirty, and she'd been up for hours.

Madison threw herself across the bed and gazed up at the ceiling tiles, counting them one by one across the perimeter of the room. In midcount, she felt her eyelids sag.

How would she ever read the Shakespeare poem at the wedding—or do anything else, for that matter?

Then, rousing herself, Madison shook off the sleepy feeling and leaped up from the bed. She headed for the shower, hoping that a little water and soap would kick-start her energy. Sure enough, by the time seven-thirty rolled around, Madison was washed, dried, powdered, combed, blow-dried, *and* energized. Now, all she needed to do was to pull on her special dress and apply her strawberry-kiwi lip gloss.

Brrrrrrrrrrrrring-a-ding!

The phone was ringing; still a little tired, Madison nearly jumped out of the terry-cloth bathrobe that had been provided by the hotel room. She lunged for the handset.

"Hello," Madison grunted.

"Now who's waking up whom?" the voice said. It was Mom.

"Actually, I've been awake since three," Madison said.

Mom gasped. "Since *three*? Good Lord! What is wrong?"

"No biggie, Mom. I just forgot to do something before and had to do it overnight, that's all. And it took me so long it didn't seem worth it to go to sleep. So I stayed up. But now—*yawn*—I am so tired. . . ."

"Of course you are!" Mom said. "Maddie, you can't just stay up all night and expect to stay awake all day. Oh, honey bear, you'll be asleep on your feet at the wedding."

"I know," Madison said, stifling another yawn.

"I'm sorry I couldn't talk last night," Mom went on. "You sounded upset. Are you feeling better? Is there something you're not telling me?"

"Well, I wish you were here," Madison admitted.

"Maddie . . ." Mom said in a comforting voice.

"And I wish that I had my own hair stylist this morning. . . ."

"Huh?" Mom asked, surprised. "What on earth are you—"

"And I wish that maybe you and Dad were still married. There, I said it."

Mom took a deep breath on the other end of the line. "Ah," she sighed. "I see."

Madison continued. "I know the Big D happened a long time ago and that it was the best thing to do and that you and Dad are happier now, but . . ."

Her voice trailed off.

"Honey bear," Mom said gently. "Change is hard. But you'll be fine. I promise—"

"Oh, Mom. Please don't promise," Madison interrupted. "Everyone is always telling me that they promise things will be good, and then something backfires, and it's a big mess, and I end up bummed out and—"

"Maddie," Mom gently interrupted again. "You'll be fine."

"That's what Dad told me," Madison said in a low whisper. She was feeling too tired to argue anymore, especially long-distance.

"Maddie, will you promise *me* something?" Mom asked.

Madison agreed reluctantly.

"Just be yourself. That's all anyone ever needs you to be," Mom said. "And remember, honey bear, that I love you."

"Oh, I love you, too," Madison said. She made a smooch noise into the phone. "And tell Phinnie that I love him, too."

"Call me when it's all over," Mom said before hanging up the phone.

Madison put down the receiver and parked herself on the bed. The clock now said seven-forty-five. She had just enough time to log on to her computer and write in her files before she got dressed for real.

223

The Wedding March

The wedding march song always sounds like "dum, dum, dee, dum" doesn't it? I was thinking about how funny that is since this wedding has me feeling like a "dum, dum, dee, dummy."

Rude Awakening: Why do they call it a wedding march when no one marches? It's not like Stephanie's coming down the aisle in her combat boots, right? I mean, Mrs. Wolfe would never go for that. LOL.

Since yours truly hasn't slept, I'll be sleepwalking through this ceremony, not marching. This isn't exactly how I imagined it would be although I guess I've been pretty pessimistic all along, haven't I? I mean, what am I really supposed to be doing here? I feel like I'm letting my friends from home down. And now I'm letting Dad down.

At least I finished the collage. Well, sort of. I meant to add this layer of glitter on one page, but it won't have time to dry. And I don't know if the poem is really as good as it could be, but it's too late to worry about that

Knock, knock, knock.
Madison glanced up from her computer.
"Dad?" Madison asked.

224

"Maddie?" Dad called out through the door. "Are you awake?"

Without turning off her laptop, Madison snapped down the cover. She hurried over to the door, clutching the sides of her terry-cloth robe, just as Dad poked his head inside her room.

"'Morning," Madison said with a grunt. She tried to shake off her sleepy state. She'd admitted the truth to Mom about having been up since three, but she didn't want Dad to know.

Dad had on jeans and a checkered shirt for now. The tuxedo would come later. Madison could see little droplets speckling his forehead. He looked pink all over, as if he were overheating.

"Hey, Maddie!"

Appearing from behind Dad, Uncle Rick and Aunt Violet came into the room, too. Madison covered herself up, blushing a little.

"Hey," she said softly, leaning in to give them a kiss. Since she hardly ever saw them, hellos always felt awkward—and being dressed in only a robe didn't help matters much.

"Are you feeling okay, Dad?" Madison asked, rubbing her own eyes. "You're not still upset about last night, are you? I mean, you're not mad at me, are you? I was acting kind of strange before, and you look kind of . . ."

"Of course I'm not mad at you!" Dad exclaimed, wiping his brow again. "I'm just dandy, except for the sweating. But then again, I always was hot stuff. . . ."

Madison giggled. "Oh, Dad."

Dad snickered to himself, which made Madison glad. He wasn't overheating—just nervous.

"Excited for your dad's big day?" Aunt Violet chirped. She was dressed in yellow from head to toe—like a canary.

Madison nodded. "Sure am," she said.

"Your dad says there have been parties all week-end," Uncle Rick said. "Sorry we missed 'em, eh?"

Madison nodded again. "Sure am," she said.

"How's school?" Aunt Violet asked.

Madison brought them up to date on life back home. Her uncle and aunt told her how much they had missed seeing Maddie at Thanksgiving. Having members of her family in the room made Madison miss her mom and friends in Far Hills even more.

"So, will I be hanging with you two today?" Madison asked them, expecting a resounding "YES!" for a reply.

Dad shook his head. "I don't think so," he said glumly. "Unfortunately, there are some conflicts. . . ."

"Oh?" Madison asked.

"I wish I could drive you over to the wedding events," Uncle Rick added. "But I have to stay with your dad, and Violet is meeting an old friend in Houston before the wedding."

"Oh," Madison said again.

"But we'll see lots of you later today," Aunt Violet chimed in.

Madison forced a smile, although she was disappointed. "Promise?" she asked.

Uncle Rick grabbed her around the shoulders and squeezed. "Absolutely!" he said. "This is a big day!"

After a few stalled good-byes, Uncle Rick and Aunt Violet headed back to their room to get a few things. Dad sat down in a swivel chair, crossed his legs, and stared out the window.

"You okay?" he asked Madison.

"I guess," Madison said. "What are you thinking about?"

"How grateful and glad I am that you're here," Dad said. "The truth is that you're my one and only, you know that? My one and only."

Madison wrapped her arms around Dad's shoulders. He was getting sappy all over again, but she didn't mind one bit.

"You're my girl," Dad said, looking a little emotional. "My little, baby girl . . ."

Madison was tempted to say, "Dad, I am *so* not little or babyish anymore. Cut that out!" But instead, she leaned in to kiss the top of his head. It was as though their roles had been reversed. And right now, he needed her comfort even more than she needed his.

"So, are you going to get dressed?" Dad asked.

Madison burst into giggles. "Dad! Of course I am.

I was going to, but then you all barged into my room. . . ."

"Sorry! Sorry!" Dad said. "I'm a little tense, I guess."

"Are you leaving now?" Madison asked.

"I have to leave, yes," Dad said in a low whisper, sounding guiltier than guilty. "Will you be okay without me or Uncle Rick and Aunt Violet?"

"Uh-huh," Madison said, trying to act upbeat. "Really!"

"So here's the plan," Dad said. "Stephanie's sister Wanda is going to pick you up. She should be here in an hour or so. Around nine, I think."

"Okay," Madison said.

"I think she'll be coming with Tiffany," Dad said. "So that's a good thing. You'll have someone to spend time with."

At that point, Madison fought the urge to scream "*Blecch*!" How could Dad have not noticed that she and Tiffany weren't exactly BFF material?

But Madison didn't scream anything. She just listened.

Dad laid out the plans for the remainder of the day, promising (more promises!) that he would try to spend as much time as possible with Madison. But Madison knew that this was probably their last private moment together before Dad turned into Mr. Married for a second time.

"I told you how much it means to have you here by my side, right?" Dad said reassuringly.

"Uh-huh," Madison said.

"And I told you that you mean the world to me, right?"

"Uh-huh."

"And I told you that—"

"Just go, Dad," Madison said. "I'm cool."

"You're always cool," Dad said, mopping his brow again. "Gee, how's about you lend your hot, sweaty dad a little of that cool?"

Madison chuckled. "Bye, Dad," she said as he disappeared through the divider door.

"Later, gator," Dad quipped. "Thank you again."

He waved and blew a kiss. Then he was gone.

Madison went back to her laptop. There wasn't much time now before Wanda arrived, and she had one more very important person to talk to before she dressed for the wedding.

From: MadFinn
To: Wetwinz
Subject: Thinking of U
Date: Sat 20 July 8:02 AM

How r things in Far Hills? Aimee
wrote and told me what happened. Is
ur Dad doing better since surgery
or whatever they're doing to fix
his heart? That was such sad news.
Are you and Chet OK?
Wow, I miss you so much, Fiona. I
know how I feel just watching my

229

dad go off and marry someone other than Mom. I feel this weird kind of empty feeling inside. It must be so hard seeing your dad sick like that.

Why am I in Texas? Grrrrr.

I should be in Far Hills RIGHT NOW. U know I LYLAS, right? I am totally, 100% here 4 u. I know that sounds pretty lame. But I mean it. I really mean it.

U probably don't have time to write or n e thing. I guess ur @ the hospital now. I will be home Sunday though and I hope I will see u right away. Can I C U right away? Right now I have to go get dressed for the wedding. I am trying sooo hard to get excited but I haven't even really practiced my poem and I don't know if I even like my dress n e more. I'll write more 18r. Talk 2 u sooner than soon.

Love,

Maddie

As soon as Madison hit SEND, there was another knock. Only this time, it came from the door that led into the main hallway.

Madison scooted over and peered through the peephole.

At first, she didn't see anyone.

But then she saw *her*. . . . standing there . . . in a perfect, pale, lavender dress.

Tiffany.

Madison grabbed the door with both hands to keep from falling over. What was she doing here—now? It wasn't nine yet! She clicked open the lock and turned the knob.

"Hello?" Madison mumbled.

"Aw, jeepers!" Tiffany said, covering her mouth so she wouldn't laugh. "You're not even ready yet?" She snapped a piece of gum. Tiffany's smile was shiny-white, her eyes ringed with purple liner and mascara, and she had on sweet-smelling perfume.

"My dad said you'd be here at nine," Madison stammered. She smelled like soap.

"Well, it's practically nine, now," Tiffany said. "Right?"

"Actually, it's not even eight-thirty," Madison said.

"Nice outfit," Tiffany joked.

"This isn't really my out—" Madison started to say. She stopped in midsentence. "I still have to get dressed."

"Whatever," Tiffany grinned. "My mom is waiting downstairs, and she said to tell you that we have lots of things to do today, and, since you're practically one of the cousins, she wants you to feel like you're part of the family, so you should come with us. Blah, blah, blah."

"Oh," Madison said.

"Yeah," Tiffany said with a toss of her head. "So, are you going to get dressed in a real dress or what?"

"Sure," Madison said. "I'll just put on my clothes and come right down to the lobby, okay?"

"Mom's in kind of a hurry," Tiffany said. "Did I say that already?"

"Yes," Madison said. She could feel her pulse quicken. "I'll hurry. I promise."

"Don't forget, we won't be coming back to the hotel, so you should bring everything you need for the wedding, all right? Mom said to tell you that, too."

"Got it," Madison said.

"What's your dress like, anyway?" Tiffany asked, poking her nose inside Madison's room.

"Well, it's not as . . . um . . . purple . . . as your dress," Madison said.

"Actually, this color is called Sweet Lavender," Tiffany corrected her. "What color are you wearing?"

"Actually, my dress is orange. . . ."

"Orange?" Tiffany let out a little gasp.

"What's wrong?" Madison gulped.

"Well," Tiffany said with another flip of her hair. "Nothing's wrong with orange if you're an orange. But . . . I never heard of an orange . . . Oh, well. Forget I said anything."

Madison could almost feel the blood drain from her face. Panicked thoughts zipped through her head like little fireflies. She had a vision of herself walking up to the wedding ceremony at the Wolfe Ranch. There, a burly cowboy bouncer would greet her.

"Hey, you in the orange dress!" he would exclaim, readying his lasso to rope Madison like loose cattle. *No orange allowed at this hoedown!*

"So . . . should I wait downstairs?" Tiffany asked, snapping her gum again.

"Yes. Can I meet you in the lobby?" Madison asked.

"I guess."

"Okay, great," Madison said. She quickly closed the door.

"Okay!" Tiffany said from behind the door.

"Sorry!" Madison cried. She struggled to re-open the door, but it stuck. Madison peered through the peephole. Was Tiffany standing there, fuming?

As it turned out, her cousin-to-be had already disappeared down the hall.

Madison stumbled away from the door and threw herself across the edge of the bed.

No orange allowed! she heard again inside her head.

Over by the closet, her junior-maid-of-honor dress was laughing at her.

Chapter 17

Madison walked calmly over to the closet and took her dress off its hanger.

Think positive thoughts, she told herself, trying to forget about the look of disgust on Tiffany's face. So what if my dress is different? So what?

Madison pulled the dress on, one foot at a time, wiggling and zipping up the side until it fit just right. Then she flipped the little ruffle at the bottom and turned to her reflection in the floor-length bathroom mirror.

After staring at the dress from every conceivable angle, Madison slipped on the orange shoes and faced the mirror again.

There were *some* positives.

For one thing, the dress was sleeveless. That way, Madison could stay cooler than cool during the ceremony. Unlike Dad, the nervous groom.

For another thing, the dress fit nicely. Madison didn't feel fat or self-conscious about the way it hung on her body.

But then there was her skin. That was a problem.

Under the bathroom lights, and wearing this orange-colored dress, Madison's face looked a little more peach-colored than usual. In the shadows, it looked downright orange. Had Mom been right when she teasingly called Madison a Creamsicle?

In the middle of everything else, Madison spotted a teeny-tiny, barely-there spot in the middle of her cheek. She picked at it, hoping it would go away. And the more she picked at it, the redder and BIGGER it got.

Think positive thoughts, Madison said to herself again. She could hear Gramma Helen's voice inside her head. Gramma was always spouting affirmations like that.

"What luck. Now I have a pimple that matches my dress," Madison said aloud, disgusted at the new development. Luckily, Mom had lent Madison her cover-up stick, so Madison was able to mask the growing pimple before it turned volcanic.

But that wasn't the only disaster.

Madison's hair didn't look right, either.

First, she pulled it back in a clip. Then, she tried a brown hair bob. Nothing looked right.

Madison tried wearing it loose on her shoulders, but that looked too messy. She didn't have hair gel or hairspray or mousse or anything to hold it in place. Frustrated, she ran a comb through the side and decided to deal with it later in the day. She still had time before the actual wedding to come up with a better hairdo.

Madison grabbed the wedding collage and carefully put it into a supersized envelope she'd bought for the occasion. On the outside of the envelope, she wrote: "For Dad and Stephanie."

The dress fit, the shoes fit, and the collage worked. But Madison felt dizzy with fatigue. How was she going to get through the morning and muddle through the reading at the wedding? She needed sleep—desperately.

Madison took a deep breath and collected everything she needed for the day: collage, book of poems, assorted hair clips, her mom's cover-up make-up (just in case), spare lip gloss, tissues, and her digital camera.

She cast one more glance at herself in the mirror and left the hotel room.

No sooner had Madison stepped off the elevator into the lobby than she spotted Tiffany and company, seated in big, sunken, upholstered chairs.

"She's *heeeeeere*," Madison heard Tiffany say as she approached.

Wanda stood up, arms extended. "Good morning,

darlin'," she said to Madison. "You look so pretty."

"Thanks," Madison said, her head down.

Wanda gave Madison a bear hug. "How did you sleep?" she asked.

Madison smiled. "Okay," she said, figuring it was better not to tell the whole world that she'd been up half the night.

"Can we go now, or what?" Tiffany whined loudly.

"Tiffany!" Wanda yelled. "Will you puh-leeze? I was just talking to Madison. . . ."

"Sorry," Tiffany said. "I was only trying to—"

"Hush!" Wanda barked.

Tiffany made a face and turned away.

"Well, I just have to gather another family friend who's staying here at the Bellville Villas," Wanda explained. "One of Stephanie's coworkers is just getting ready. She said she'd be a few minutes. I'm just going to go get her. You gals wait right here, okay?"

"How long do we have to wait now?" Tiffany asked.

Wanda grabbed Tiffany by the elbow and pulled her away from where they'd been standing. Madison could hear their frantic whispers—but just barely.

"You behave, young lady!" Wanda cautioned her daughter.

"Mother, please. You're embarrassing me," Tiffany said.

"Hush up!" Wanda cried. "I expect you to behave

238

and act like a perfect young miss today. There will be no complaining. Do you hear me?"

Tiffany pulled her elbow back and rubbed it. "That hurts," she said.

Wanda grabbed it again. "I don't care. Now, behave!"

"Can we go into the arcade room over there and wait?" Tiffany asked.

Wanda shook her head. "No way," she said. "Not after this display of yours this morning."

"But it's only for a few—" Tiffany began.

"I said no!" Wanda said firmly.

"What if Madison wants to go?" Tiffany asked.

"I don't care. I said no," Wanda said. "Sit down and quit it."

Madison looked away quickly so she wouldn't be caught eavesdropping.

As soon as her mother had walked away, Tiffany turned around. "I am so embarrassed," she said aloud.

"What happened?" Madison asked.

"Let's go into the video arcade. She won't be back for ten minutes," Tiffany said.

"But I thought—" Madison cut herself off. She didn't know what to say. She'd clearly heard Wanda warn Tiffany *not* to go inside the arcade.

"Are you coming?" Tiffany groaned. She turned toward the arcade entrance. "Don't worry. I have quarters."

Madison followed Tiffany into the small room,

where four video machines were up against one wall, two pinball machines against another, with a ping-pong table in the middle.

"This is lame," Tiffany said. "But it beats sitting in the lobby."

Madison nodded. "Yeah."

And it did.

For five minutes, Madison stood behind Tiffany, as her cousin-to-be pummeled a pinball machine.

"You got a million points already!" Madison said excitedly. "You're a pro!"

Tiffany smiled. "Look out!"

Madison cheered her on.

"I'm really sorry you had a fight with your mom," Madison said after another minute.

"It's, like, her job or something to make me feel like I'm . . . oh, I don't know. I just wish she'd lay off," Tiffany groaned.

Madison nodded in agreement, even though, right now, she actually missed her own mom.

"By the way, that dress is the deal," Tiffany said, examining Madison's outfit. "I never would have guessed that orange could look so cool."

Madison pulled away, surprised. "You think so?" she said.

"I should dress more like you," Tiffany said.

"Like *me*?" Madison said.

"Yeah!" Tiffany said. "I'm always stuck in outfits my mother picks for me. I mean, I like this one, but sometimes she makes me wear these hideous dresses that Grandma Diane wouldn't even wear. . . ."

"I think you look great," Madison said.

Tiffany laughed out loud. "Well, maybe. I know at least my hair looks good. And it's not just because I went to this stylist. . . ."

Madison wanted to laugh. Tiffany sounded so stuck-up! But she wasn't anything like Poison Ivy, Madison realized. She said outrageous things, but she seemed not to mean to come across as self-absorbed or cruel. She was just really into hairdos and dressing up. . . .

And pinball.

"I always wanted blond hair like yours," Madison said, tossing her own locks. "Sometimes my hair can be so scary. Look at it. I still don't know what to do with it for the wedding."

Tiffany nodded and inspected Madison's hairdo. "It does look as if it's just lying there."

Madison made a face. "Gee, thanks."

"Aw! Don't get all huffy," Tiffany said. She raised a finger to her lip-glossed lips as though she were thinking extra hard. "How about flowers?"

"Flowers?" Madison said.

"Add 'em to your hair. Like a dancer or a model," Tiffany said. "Flowers would look super good, don't you think?"

Madison shrugged. "I don't know what to think anymore. . . ."

"Okay, look. Here's the story. I have the best hair clip in the whole world, and it's orange-red, and it would match *perfectly!*" Tiffany squealed. "We have to get that for you, now."

"Now?" Madison asked, in disbelief.

In a matter of moments, Stephanie's niece had turned into Madison's fashion adviser.

How had that happened?

Madison gave in to Tiffany's makeover tips. "You're being so nice to me," she said.

Tiffany rolled her eyes. "That's right. We have to stick together now. We're cousins, right?"

Madison grinned. So far, today, she liked having new cousins—a lot.

"So, are you close to Aunt Steph or what?" Tiffany asked. "You never say much about what y'all do back North."

"Stephanie is nice," Madison said. "We see each other a lot."

"Did you know that Aunt Stephanie is, like, the only person in our entire family who left Texas?" Tiffany said. "Does she talk about us, ever?"

"Oh, sure," Madison said. "All the time," she added, exaggerating a little.

"Usually, she'd take us to all these places when she came home," Tiffany said. "But I have this feeling she won't be visiting Texas as much anymore."

"No?" Madison asked.

Tiffany shrugged. "Well, of course not. She has this whole life with you and your dad up there. Why would she bother coming back here?"

"Maybe she'll just get homesick," Madison said.

"Yeah. Sick of home," Tiffany joked.

"But she loves Texas," Madison said.

Tiffany shrugged. "She loves her job and your dad. That's all I know."

"And everyone in your family," Madison said. "It's so big."

"Mammoth," Tiffany said. "We have a mammoth family. That's what Kirk always says."

Madison giggled.

All at once, Tiffany took Madison by the arm and pulled her out of the arcade and into the lobby. She motioned toward the elevators. Wanda had reappeared, followed by a gray-haired woman wearing a dark-green pant suit.

"How did you know your mom was coming?" Madison asked.

Tiffany raised her eyebrows. "Wanda radar," she joked. "That's what Kirk calls it."

Wanda swept toward them.

"Gals, this is Ms. Morgan," Wanda announced. "Did I get that right?" she asked Ms. Morgan, who nodded, waiting for her cue to speak.

"So, it's just us girls, huh?" Ms. Morgan said.

Madison smiled back. "Yup."

Tiffany tossed her hair. "Mom," she said to Wanda

in her sweetest voice. "Can we swing back by the house? I forgot something."

"What now?" Wanda said.

Tiffany turned toward Madison. "Oh, nothing much," she said. "Just this hair clip that I really need."

Madison's eyes opened wide. Tiffany was asking Wanda to stop home for *her*? She couldn't believe it.

"Fine," Wanda conceded. "We'll swing by the house. But for one minute *only*," she grumbled.

The morning had taken a new twist.

Tiffany wasn't poison at all. And she wasn't a goody-goody, either. Madison was sure now that, if she could keep her eyes open, perhaps Dad and Stephanie's wedding might turn out all right after all.

The group of four piled into Wanda's car and hit the road.

The first stop was Rhona's Roadside Diner—for food.

The second stop: Pump-N-Dash Gas—for fuel.

The third stop: Wanda's house—for the hair clip.

Madison couldn't believe it when they pulled into Tiffany's driveway.

"It looks like a house you'd see in some magazine," Madison said aloud, without realizing she was speaking.

Wanda laughed. "You think? *Nawwww*."

"Mother," Tiffany groaned from the backseat. "We have one of the bigger ones in the neighborhood, right?"

Madison chuckled to herself. Once again, Tiffany

sounded stuck-up, but she wasn't really that way at all. Madison was pretty sure that Tiffany had no idea she came across any other way but nice.

"Your place sure is bigger than our house back in Far Hills," Madison said.

"What are you waiting for, Tiff? Get inside, and make it quick!" Wanda ordered.

Tiffany leaped out of the car and sped to the front door of the house. While they were waiting for her to reappear with the hair clip, Wanda and Ms. Morgan began chatting.

Madison opened up the book of poems and quietly read the wedding selection Dad and Stephanie had selected. Madison wished that she had memorized the poem so she wouldn't have had to keep sneaking peeks at the page.

Madison was very glad that in a couple of hours, the whole poem thing would be ancient history.

From Wanda's house, the foursome drove on toward the ranch for the big event. In the backseat, Tiffany opened a small lavender bag (which matched her dress, of course) and produced the hair clip she had picked up at the house, along with bobby pins, hairspray, and a giant, round brush.

"I think we should pinch the edges a little and tease it here," Tiffany said, waving her hands around Madison's head. She handed Madison a small mirror. "Look for yourself."

Madison didn't see what the fuss was about. She

didn't have a clue about hairdos. "Are you sure?" she asked.

Tiffany pursed her lips. "It's going to look *gooooood*," she said in a long drawl.

Madison closed her eyes and surrendered. She figured that no one with such perfect blond hair could mess it up. Less than ten minutes later, after spritzing and spraying and pulling, Tiffany was ready to celebrate her hairdo masterpiece.

"Ta-da!" Tiffany announced from the backseat.

"Well you certainly used enough hairspray!" Wanda declared, pinching her nose.

"Madison Finn!" Ms. Morgan turned around to look, too. "You look like a different person!"

"See? Told you." Tiffany had a self-satisfied smirk on her face.

Madison grabbed the mirror. She saw the teased and flipped 'do she could never have done in a zillion years by herself.

"Oh, Tiffany," Madison gushed. "I love it. And the hair clip really is perfect."

Wanda let out a big laugh from the front seat. "So I guess this settles it, then, hon," she called back to Tiffany. "Hairdressing school for you. Those stylists have taught you a thing or two, eh?"

"Aw, Mother," Tiffany whined.

Madison didn't let their banter ruin the moment. Despite being very tired, her new look was giving her a good feeling.

She couldn't wait to show off her hair and dress to Dad and the others.

By ten-thirty that morning, when Wanda zipped into the driveway at Wolfe Ranch, it was brimming with wedding guests. Some had pulled up in trucks, others in minivans. A few had even come by horse, Madison guessed. There were a few ponies tethered out in front of the mansion.

"Grandma always puts out the animals and dresses people up in costumes. . . ." Tiffany explained. "She's way over the top, know what I mean?"

Madison giggled, because she hadn't met a single person there in Bellville who *wasn't* over the top. Real or not, Madison was in awe of the spectacle. She wondered what Aimee and Fiona would have thought of all of it.

Mrs. Wolfe had a waitstaff that ran around taking care of all such details as the parking of cars, taking of bags and coats, and directing of traffic. Every single person was wearing the same type of white shirt, colored bandana, suede pants, and cowboy boots; it was like some kind of wedding uniform.

"Hey!" a voice called out as Tiffany and Madison climbed out of the backseat of Wanda's car.

Madison turned to see Kirk coming across the driveway.

"What's up?" Kirk asked. "We wondered when you were getting here."

"Hello, Captain Kirk," Tiffany joked. "Madison and I are having the best morning ever, Cuz. What were *you* doing?"

Madison stood back, smiling silently.

"Well, it's way too hot to wear a suit," Kirk complained.

Tiffany pretended to fan herself. "Gotcha. That's why I'm glad this dress has thin straps."

Madison stared at Kirk as he started to crack one joke after the next. His hair looked very good. Madison wondered if maybe he, too, had gotten styling advice from Tiffany.

"Madison, I dig your dress," Kirk commented as they walked together toward the house. "It's retro or something, right?"

"Oh," Madison said. She felt her cheeks flush. "You like it?"

"What about *my* dress?" Tiffany wailed.

"Yeah. Didn't you wear that dress at Cousin Betta's wedding?" Kirk asked his cousin.

"What?" Tiffany barked. "I never, ever, *ever* wear the same dress twice to a family function. . . ."

Kirk laughed out loud. He turned to Madison. "Like I would remember what she ever wore to anything!" he cracked. "I was kidding, Tiff. Take a chill pill."

Tiffany's expression turned to a scowl. "I'm going

to get you back for that one, Kirk!" she said, chasing him inside.

Madison dropped back a little to see if she could spot Dad anywhere among the crowd. Right now, she wanted to see him more than anyone else.

"Madison!" Tiffany cried. "Are you coming, or what?"

Madison nodded and followed Tiffany and Kirk inside. She glanced around the entryway to look at the hanging lanterns and the candles. It looked completely different from the way it had just one day earlier. Guests milled about, admiring the decor, including the family collection of steer antlers and woven rugs.

Madison couldn't believe that Dad had said the wedding would ever be just fifteen or even thirty people. There were at least ten times that many guests standing in this room alone!

Tiffany came running over. "Madison," she whispered. "You have to come with me. Quick!"

"Huh? Where?" Madison asked.

"It's a secret," Tiffany said.

She led Madison out through the back sliding doors onto a patio covered with bales of hay and branding irons and a giant sculpture of a bull. Some of the younger cousins took turns climbing on the bull's back. On one side of the house, a huge Texas flag made out of flowers was displayed.

Madison giggled. She always imagined weddings

249

as affairs of white tablecloths and lace. This was more like a movie set with lots of props.

"Where are you taking me?" she asked Tiffany again.

"You'll see!" Tiffany said. "You'll see!"

Tiffany led Madison through the courtyard into the open area where they had had the rehearsal the day before. Today it was to be the site of the main ceremony. Horseshoes had been hung up and down the length of the split-wood fence that surrounded the area. Hundreds of chairs with backs shaped like horseshoes were lined up together. One giant horseshoe painted with the words *Wolfe Ranch* hung over the altar where the wedding service was to be held.

Off to the side, Madison saw a small tent. Tiffany headed straight for it.

"Isn't this place for food?" Madison asked, almost tripping over her Creamsicle-colored shoes.

"Shhhhh!" Tiffany said, lifting the hem of her lavender dress.

Madison followed her inside.

The tent didn't contain catering equipment or lights. On one side was a huge mirror. Standing before it was Stephanie, tugging on her long, white dress edged in lace.

She looked more beautiful than Madison could have imagined.

Sonnet XVIII ❧

William Shakespeare

Shall I compare thee to a summer's day?
Thou art more lovely and more temperate:
Rough winds do shake the darling buds of May,
And summer's lease hath all too short a date:
Sometime too hot the eye of heaven shines,
And often is his gold complexion dimmed,
And every fair from fair sometime declines,
By chance, or nature's changing course untrimmed:
But thy eternal summer shall not fade,
Nor lose possession of that fair thou ow'st,
Nor shall death brag thou wander'st in his shade,
When in eternal lines to time thou grow'st,
So long as men can breathe, or eyes can see,
So long lives this, and this gives life to thee.

Chapter 18

Madison felt a bead of sweat trickle down her back. She wriggled around and pretended it wasn't there as she stared out into the sea of people before her.

Off to the left, Dad beamed. Uncle Rick, who was standing to Dad's left, grinned just as broadly. Stephanie looked ready to wipe a tear from her eye. In the first row, even Stephanie's mother was quietly paying attention. Sitting nearby, Aunt Violet gave a big thumbs-up to Madison.

Madison read the last line of the poem slowly. *"So long lives this, and this gives life to thee."*

Everyone let out a collective sigh. Tiffany tossed her hair. Kirk stuck out his tongue as if he were going to throw up. But Madison didn't mind.

That was exactly like what Egg would have done.

Madison turned toward Dad again. He was looking in her direction. She bit her lip as if to say, "So?" and Dad nodded proudly.

"Great job," Dad said softly, mouthing the words to Madison.

Madison returned to her seat. The sweat kept trickling, but she didn't mind. The worst part was way over. And her hair still looked great.

The minister asked everyone to rise for a blessing and then to be seated once again for the final vows. The bride and groom each recited their vows after the minister prompted them.

"I, Stephanie Mae Wolfe, take thee, Jeffrey Peter Finn, to be my wedded husband. . . ."

Stephanie didn't say anything else for a split second. The entire crowd in the backyard seemed to hold its breath in unison. Madison leaned forward and grabbed the chair in front of her.

What was wrong? Had Stephanie forgotten the words? Was she about to run away and leave Dad?

All at once, Stephanie spoke.

"To have and to hold, from this day forward . . ." Stephanie continued. "For better or for worse . . . for richer or for poorer . . . in sickness and in health . . . to love and to cherish . . . till death do us part."

The minister turned to Dad and asked him to repeat the same vows. Dad looked more nervous than Madison had ever seen him.

Behind the area where Dad and Stephanie stood, the sun shone brightly over the wide ranch, like a picture postcard. Madison reached into her bag for the digital camera and snapped a photo.

"I, Jeffrey Peter Finn . . ." Dad said slowly, "take thee, Stephanie Mae Wolfe, to be my lawful wedded husband . . . I mean, awful wedded wife . . . I mean . . ."

Madison's eyes bugged out.

What was Dad doing?

The minister just smiled. "Take your time," he said gently.

Madison saw Stephanie squeeze Dad's hand in reassurance.

Dad wiped his brow. "To be my lawful . . . wed-ded . . . wife . . ."

The entire wedding party started to clap. The minister held up his hand for everyone to hush. Dad continued.

"To have and to hold, from this day forward . . . for better or for worse . . . for richer or for poorer . . . in sickening health . . ."

Dad threw his hands up into the air.

"In sickness . . . and . . . in . . . health!" he corrected himself. "To love and to cherish . . . till death do us part."

Stephanie's shoulders shook. At first Madison thought she might be crying, but then she knew for sure that her new stepmother was laughing—hysterically.

254

"Is she okay?" someone behind Madison mumbled.

Of course, Madison knew Stephanie was just fine.

This was love, that was all. Love of the kind Dad had described to Madison the night before.

"By the power vested in me by the state of Texas, I now pronounce you husband and wife. . . ." the minister said.

Someone in the crowd yelled "*Yahoo!*" Madison's heart thumped. This really was romantic. She snapped another picture.

"You may kiss the bride!" another person yelled from the back of the crowd.

"Yeah, kiss her!"

A loud cheer arose from the guests. Everyone jumped to his or her feet, stomping and yelling. Madison swallowed hard. She wasn't too crazy about watching Dad kiss anyone.

Madison had spent so many hours worrying about the dress, the poem, and, most of all—Dad. Yet it had taken only twenty minutes for everything to change.

Everything.

As soon as the music started up for Dad and Stephanie's walk back down the aisle, Madison pushed her way through a cluster of people. She wanted to catch Dad and congratulate him. She wanted to see for herself what was different about him, now that he was married again. Madison needed to make sure Dad was still the same old Dad who loved her and considered *her* his one and only. After all, that was what he'd said just last night.

But the crowd of people blocked Madison's view and she couldn't wave high enough or yell loud enough to grab Dad's attention. She watched helplessly as he whisked his new bride back down the makeshift aisle. Madison couldn't even reach her uncle and aunt.

"Can you see, darlin'?" a woman in a bright, yellow hat asked Madison.

Madison nodded. "Uh-huh." But she couldn't really see anything at all. How could Dad just *dash*? Madison wondered. She wanted to run away, too. She would have run, if she hadn't been in Texas.

"You did such a fine, fine job at that poem," the woman said. "Your daddy must be as pleased as punch."

"I guess so," Madison said, her eyes still searching for Dad.

She looked around for Kirk and Tiffany, too, but they seemed to have vanished permanently.

"Madison!"

Madison heard Wanda call out from a few rows back, where she'd been chatting up some other guests. "What are you doing all by yourself?" Wanda asked. "Come here, and meet Stephanie's cousin from Albuquerque."

Madison smiled meekly and pushed her way through a couple of rows of chairs to reach Wanda. She shook the cousin's hand (just how many cousins did Stephanie have, anyhow?) and tried to pay attention as he spoke.

Then someone else shouted her name.

"Madison!"

Madison turned quickly when she realized that Kirk was the one who was calling her. He beckoned Madison over to where he was standing. She excused herself from Wanda and the other cousin and made her way to him.

"Where did you disappear?" Madison asked.

"Tiff wanted to see Aunt Steph for a sec. Did you talk to your dad? He was looking for you."

"He was?" Madison said. She grinned. "I thought he forgot I was even here."

"No way," Kirk said. "Your dad and your uncle Rick were looking everywhere for you. I guess they wanted to get some photos or something."

"Photos? I have to find them," Madison said.

"Yeah, sure," Kirk said. "I'll see you at the tables, okay? Aunt Wanda told me that she made sure we all sat near each other. Should be cool."

"Thanks so much, Kirk," Madison said sweetly. "I mean . . . Cousin." She threw her arms around him.

"Um . . . sure. No problemo," Kirk said, not really hugging back. The dumbstruck look on his face said it all. He didn't know what to do.

257

Madison backed off with a smile. "See ya," she said, disappearing to look for Dad. She didn't know what had inspired her to hug her cute new cousin, but she had. Madison chuckled to herself as she walked away. If only she had had the guts to reach out and hug someone else she really liked—like Hart.

Now *that* would have been something.

"I can't believe this was ever considered a small wedding," Dad said, squeezing Madison around the waist. "Look at this crazy mess!"

"I know," Madison said. "I couldn't find you for ages."

Dad kissed her on the top of her head. "I will never be very far away, honey bear," Dad said. "I promise."

This time, Madison believed his promise.

Madison marveled at the display of food. Stephanie's family had outdone themselves. This was a real, live hoedown, complete with every Texas dish imaginable. The plates were all marked with clever names that tied in to the wedding theme, from Hoedown Hickory–smoked Bison Sausage and Texas Two-pot Beef Chili to Wedding Bells Chicken Fried Steak and Stephanie Mae Jambalaya. There were pinto beans, okra, corn bread, coleslaw, cobbler, and about twelve different kinds of hot sauce to put on top on top of things.

Madison stood over the buffet table, plate in hand, and inhaled deeply. She'd been to plenty of barbecues before, but nothing like this. It was a far cry from the BBQ celebrations Drew Maxwell had at his house.

"So, what do you think?" Dad asked.

"I thought this would be some fancy party," Madison said. "But it's more like a rodeo or something. I mean, Kirk told me there are games and pony rides."

"Stephanie wanted this to be fun for all the kids," Dad explained. "Isn't that great?" His eyes danced when he pronounced Stephanie's name.

"You look really happy, Dad," Madison said.

"I am happy," Dad said. "I'm happy you're here, Maddie."

"No, I mean about being married again. I understand now why you wanted to marry Stephanie. Things are different now—but in a good way," Madison said.

"In a VERY good way," Dad said with a wink. "Look, honey bear, I hate to run off on you again today, but I have to go around and visit with some other guests. Will you be okay?"

Madison nodded. "Sure, Dad. I understand."

"Save me a square dance, okay?" Dad said.

Madison's jaw dropped. "Um . . . I don't think so, Dad," she said with a giggle. "I am not dancing."

"We'll see about that," Dad said. He hustled off

to another table, where Stephanie was waiting to introduce him to another crowd of family friends.

Someone clinked a glass, and the whole room stopped to watch Dad and Stephanie kiss again.

"Is that really necessary?" Kirk said, coming up behind Madison with Tiffany.

"You are totally unromantic, Kirk," Tiffany said.

"And that's a *good* thing!" Kirk cracked himself up with his remark.

The band played a string of country tunes and then broke into a set of old-time rock and roll. Dad and Stephanie bounced onto the dance floor together while everyone watched.

Madison stared at her new stepmother and her new dad as they moved across the dance floor together, arms interlocked, legs moving in perfect rhythm.

Tiffany stood next to Madison, knees bouncing as if she were dying to dance, too.

"This is so awesome," Tiffany observed. "I have never seen my Aunt Steph so happy."

"Really?" Madison asked.

"My mom always told me Aunt Steph was way into her job and traveling, and that she never dated that many guys, except for this one guy Bob. She was supposed to get married to him, I think. But they called it off. I'm glad they did. Your dad is way nicer than Bob ever was."

"Thanks," Madison said.

Tiffany nodded. "Well, that's what my mom says."

Madison glanced back at Stephanie and Dad again. Her stepmother pulled a part of the train off the back of her dress—it was detachable for dancing! She kicked off her white shoes, too. The band played a few more dance tunes.

Another one of Tiffany's cousins came over and asked Tiffany to dance. Without a moment's hesitation, she wiggled away in her lavender dress, leaving Madison alone.

Madison got herself a cup of punch from the table.

"Fiona!" someone called out across the dance floor.

Instinctively, Madison turned to see who had uttered the cry. She saw two people she didn't know. She wondered where *her* Fiona was right now.

Was Fiona asleep in a chair at the hospital or seated by Mr. Waters's bedside, patiently waiting for word on his condition? Madison felt guilty, standing there among the two-steppers and the cowboy cooks, playing wedding guest. As soon as the party was over, Madison would send Fiona an e-mail to see what was happening back home.

Another clink sounded.

Dad waved his arms into the air and raised his own glass to the crowd.

"Thank you, everyone, for being here!" Dad cheered.

Stephanie seconded his remark. "From the bottom of our hearts."

"Here, here!" a few guests shouted.

"Stephanie Mae finally gets her man!" a woman called out from one of the side tables. That comment had Stephanie laughing. Then Dad leaned in to kiss her once again.

Madison sat down on one of the folding chairs at her table.

"Well, don't you look gorgeous!"

Aunt Violet slid into the chair next to Madison with a drink in her hand.

"Where's Uncle Rick?" Madison asked.

"Off requesting some song he wants to dance to," Aunt Violet said cheerily. "Are you having a good time?"

Madison nodded. "Sure," she said.

From across the dance floor, Uncle Rick motioned to Aunt Violet to come and dance. She stood up with a twirl and moved toward him. No sooner had she disappeared than Kirk came over and parked himself next to Madison.

"Well, you look bored," he commented.

"No way," Madison said, a bit defensively. "I'm not bored. I was just thinking."

"What about?" Kirk asked.

"Oh, you don't want to know," Madison said with a smile. "I guess, in a way, I'm relieved that this is over."

The band ended a slow song and started up with a faster, twangy, guitar number.

Kirk jumped up. "Do you want to dance?" he asked Madison.

"Me?" Madison asked. "Um . . . not exactly . . ."

"Come on," Kirk said. "You have to dance. I can't go out there alone. What's your prob? We don't have to do a slow dance or anything."

Madison giggled. "I know *that*," she said.

Kirk just shrugged. He put his hand out again. "Come on," he urged.

Madison stood up and took her cousin's hand. "I am the worst dancer on the planet, I swear," Madison said.

Kirk didn't seem to care. He wasn't really that good a dancer, either. He shook his hips a little and moved stiffly from side to side. Madison was grateful that he didn't move too much. She was having a little trouble keeping her balance in the Creamsicle-colored shoes.

The best part about dancing with Kirk was that the dance floor proved to be a *much* better place to see the wedding "action."

On the other side of the party, Tiffany was talking to a group of girls dressed in pale purple and pink dresses similar to her own. Madison guessed that the girls were probably some of her other new cousins.

Her eyes quickly searched the crowd for Dad and

Stephanie. Over by one of the Texas steer ice sculptures, Madison spotted Stephanie dishing some food onto a plate and talking to four different people at once. Uncle Rick and Aunt Violet were still dancing nearby. On the other side of the room, Wally was smoking a cigar with a bunch of men in cowboy hats.

As the song ended, Madison turned to Kirk. "This is my first hoedown," she said.

Kirk cracked up. "Don't worry. You'll get over it," he joked. "See you later."

He turned and raced across the dance floor to a cluster of other cousins. Madison returned to her chair at one of the tables to take a break from dancing.

"Excuse me, is this seat taken?"

Dad appeared and sat down in the folding chair next to Madison.

"Where were you?" she asked. "I thought you needed to say hello to all of the guests."

"I did," Dad said. "Sort of. Now it's your turn again. I promised not to desert you, right? Enjoying the hoedown?"

"Yup," Madison said.

"I saw you and Kirk on the dance floor. You and your new cousins seem to be getting along great," Dad said.

"Yeah," Madison said. "I didn't know what to think at first, but they're really nice."

"Have you played any of the games?"

Madison shook her head. "Not really, Dad. Those are for the younger kids. I'm a little beyond the hay hunt, don't you think?"

"Well . . ." Dad said awkwardly. "I guess. If you say so."

"Plus, I'm all dressed up, Dad. I can't exactly use a squirt gun in this dress. . . ."

"Okay. Well, where's my square dance?" Dad asked. He stood up and wiggled his hips.

"Dad, let's get this straight. You can't square-dance or any other kind of dance!" Madison said.

"Who says?" Dad said, grabbing Madison's wrist. "Let's find out."

"No," Madison squealed. She dragged her feet as Dad tried to yank her out onto the dance floor.

"Daddy, no!" Madison said, half laughing. "I mean it."

"Come on, honey bear," Dad said, with another goofy swivel of the hips.

"Dad, please, I really, really, *really*—"
Thwomp.

With one not-so-smooth motion, Madison's shoes wobbled, and her legs gave way underneath her, and she landed with a loud thump on the middle of the dance floor.

Madison's ankle throbbed. The room was spinning.

"Are you okay?" Dad asked.

"Oh, no," Madison said meekly. "My right foot . . . it's a little bit . . ."

Dad leaned over to pick her up.

"Ouch . . . eeee!" Madison cried.

She looked down at her ankle. It had already swelled up around the sides of one of her orange shoes.

Chapter 19

"Wanna dance again?" Kirk cracked himself up.

Madison just shook her head. "Very funny, Kirk," she said, readjusting her sitting position. She'd been propped up on a chair on one of the patios over-looking Bobcat Lake. Her ankle was wrapped in bandages and ice to keep it from swelling any more than it already had.

All around Madison, the hoedown continued with its loud music and even louder guests. Stephanie had some wild friends and family who liked to hoot and holler whenever a song they liked was being played. There was a lot of commotion near the lake, too, because Mr. Wolfe had planned for fireworks to close out the evening, and the kids at the party were eager for that to happen. A few men made preparations to row out in small boats and set up the display. As soon as the sun set, the Wolfe family promised, the "under the stars" part of the hoedown would begin. That was hours away, Madison realized. This wedding seemed to go on forever.

At first, Madison felt self-conscious about her accident. But then she saw it as an opportunity really to take in the wedding and all of its sights and sounds. Much to her surprise, she discovered that she liked watching the action from the patio. And she liked the fact that everyone was coming by to say hello.

Kirk was only one of many visitors. Almost all of her new boy and girl cousins came over to see how Madison was recuperating, in addition to seeing just how much her ankle had swollen. Was it the size of a cantaloupe or just the size of an orange? In some ways, it made Madison just another ranch attract-ion at the hoedown, but she didn't mind. She just hoped the kids wouldn't start climbing on her the way they'd been climbing on the stuffed bull earlier in the day.

For the 'first time since the weekend had begun, Madison felt as though she were a part of something. She wasn't alone anymore.

From her perch on the patio, she watched guests whirl each other around in different variations on the Texas Two-Step. She spied Stephanie dancing with a group of her girlfriends in the middle of the floor, shaking her arms like a chicken. Uncle Rick and Aunt Violet were the best whirlers of all, but Madison knew that that was because they had once been Canadian dance champions.

Suddenly Tiffany appeared. "Want some dessert, Madison?" she asked. "The waiters just put everything out on the buffet. You have to try the blackberry cobbler. Or maybe the peach pie . . ."

"Mmmm," Madison smiled. "If you don't mind getting me a piece . . ."

"No prob! Back in a flash," Tiffany said. She hustled over to the buffet table.

Dad kept checking in to see how Madison was feeling. She figured that he felt guiltier than guilty for yanking her onto the dance floor when she'd been resisting so fiercely.

"Blame me," Dad moaned. "I ruined the party for you, I know it."

"No, Dad," Madison insisted. "I'm okay. I feel fine up here."

"But you're in pain," Dad said. "And you can't dance or join in the party!"

"Exactly," Madison said with a grin. "I can't dance. That's the good part."

Dad chuckled. "Oh, I see. This was all a strategic ploy to get out of a square dance with me. Hmm."

"Yeah, me and my master plans . . ." Madison said with a laugh.

"Have you seen Uncle Rick?" Dad asked.

"Yes, and Aunt Violet has been super sweet, too," Madison said. "She and I made a promise that we'd try to keep in better touch from now on. I'm so glad they came to the wedding."

Dad smiled. "I'm glad, too. Did you talk to my work friends at all?"

"Yup," Madison said. "I met the couple from California and the guy who works in New York. Everyone has treated me like I'm royalty or something. I can't believe I've been sitting up here for almost two hours."

"Time flies when you're . . . trapped in a chair with a bum ankle," Dad joked.

"Where's Stephanie?" Madison asked.

"Off carousing," Dad said with a smirk. "She's having a blast. She came over to see you, too, right?"

"Like five times," Madison said.

"Gee whiz. What a trip," Dad said. "One surprise after another. Your mother will have my head for this one."

"No, she won't," Madison said.

Dad rolled his eyes. "You don't know your mother," he said.

"I know she just wants me to be happy. And the same goes for you."

Dad laughed. "Oh, yeah?" he asked. "She wants me to be happy? On my wedding day?"

"That's what she told me," Madison said. "Seriously. So did Gramma Helen."

"Your mother is a special woman," Dad said, choking up a little.

Madison felt a twisting sensation in her tummy. "I'm sorry for acting so weird about the wedding. Really sorry."

Dad shook his head. "Not at all, honey bear. You're allowed to feel weird when your dad gets married for a second time. Trust me. I think you've been a real trooper, especially tonight."

"I guess," Madison said. She gazed off at the lake.

Maybe it didn't look so murky anymore.

In fact, the lake—and everything around it— looked brighter than bright. The setting sun caused oranges and yellows to be reflected off the surface of the water. Bird feathers glistened. The sides of the little rowboats sparkled.

"One piece of cobbler!" Tiffany announced as she brought Madison her dessert.

"Well, I see you have your servants bringing in the supplies," Dad joked.

"Oh, Dad! Cut it out," she said, giving Dad's shoulder a little smack. "Thanks, Tiffany."

"Would you two excuse me while I go find my new bride?" Dad asked.

"Of course," Tiffany chirped. She tossed her blond hair and took a seat next to Madison's. "I'll hang out here."

"You're a great cousin," Madison said.

"Thanks. So are you." Tiffany said.

"Well, thanks," Madison said.

"Look at him!" Tiffany said all of a sudden. "He must be someone Aunt Steph works with. Do you see that scary-looking cowboy over there with the toupee? And what about that woman wearing the turquoise turban or whatever it is? Someone needs to give her a serious makeover."

Madison couldn't stop laughing at Tiffany's comments. "Aren't you related to half these people?"

"I am *not* related to *them*, no way!" Tiffany said with a growl of disgust.

"Wow. I hate to think what you thought of what I was wearing when you first met me," Madison said.

"Oh, that isn't the same thing," Tiffany said. "What did you think of *me*?"

"Well . . ." Madison flushed a little. She had to lie. "I wanted to get to know you. . . . You were so nice."

"Aw, that is sooooo sweet," Tiffany said. "Actually, I know most people think I'm too nice. Isn't that funny?"

"Hilarious," Madison said.

"Oh, look!" Tiffany said, pointing up at the sky.

The sun's luster had begun to fade, and now the colors in the sky were changing to varying shades of pink. The wedding day was slowly turning into night.

"Madison, I'm going to go find my mom," Tiffany said. "Will you still be here when I get back?"

272

Madison looked down at her foot. "Um . . ."

"Oh, yeah. Duh! Your foot," Tiffany giggled. "Okay, so I'll see you real soon, then."

Tiffany bounced away toward the dance floor and toward Kirk and the other party action, while Madison stayed put, wondering what Mom would have said if she had seen this place. She'd probably have made some funny crack about Tiffany's being a space cadet or a little bit snotty.

And what would Aimee have thought? She'd have been in heaven with all the dancing, so there would have been no time for her to think. Fiona would have liked it the best, though. Fiona was always up for an adventure.

Madison realized how much she missed Far Hills. The Texas crew was nice, but it wasn't the same thing as her friends from home.

Madison's eyes focused back on the rose-colored sky. The band played a slower song now.

Loooove, soft as an easy chair . . .

Dad and Stephanie waltzed among the other guests, arms wrapped tightly around each other's waists and shoulders.

Loooove, fresh as the morning air . . .

Madison's upper body swayed back and forth to the rhythm of the music, too, even though she didn't like the sappy song very much. It reminded her of the music that was piped into the dentist's office.

273

Slowly, the sky grew dim and turned more of a gray color. All around, couples pressed closer together. People held hands and wandered off for romantic sundown walks around the ranch. Even the ponies that were grazing from behind the fences seemed to mellow out as dusk set in.

Madison was thinking about love, too.

Back home—where her *Hart* was.

Later, after Uncle Rick had driven her back to the Bellville Villas, Madison poured her heart out into a new file. The wedding had officially ended (for her, anyway). Once again, she was writing on her laptop.

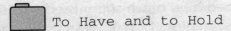 To Have and to Hold

When someone says "to have and to hold," it usually means to love someone forever. Right? When Dad said that to Stephanie today, that's what he meant. It doesn't mean to have and to hold your breath, hold your horses, or hold your nose. And it certainly doesn't mean to have and to hold a giant ice pack on your ankle.

Then again, this is ME we're talking about.

Rude Awakening: If aspirin works on a headache, then what kind of medicine helps someone like me, who's lovesick? The ice pack just isn't cutting it.

My ankle will survive, I know. But this

274

whole wedding thing had me thinking sooo hard as I sat there tonight on the patio watching all the other guests. It got me thinking about love and how I would give anything if someone would just fall in love with ME just for five minutes even. Five minutes! Is that so much to ask? Five lousy minutes!

I always tell Fiona that she's crazy to be crushing on Egg because, well, Egg is a big geek. But really, I'm jealous of them. Soooo jealous. And I'm jealous of Drew, too, because now he has his neighbor Elaine. AND I am jealous of Aimee because every boy at FHJH (including the older ones) wants to go out with her even if she only has eyes for that brainiac Ben Buckley.

Then there's me, Queen of the Ice Pack.

I wonder what Hart is doing right now at this very second? Could he be thinking of me at the exact same time that I am thinking about him?

Nah. He's probably hanging with Poison Ivy or one of his other guy friends.

Madison wriggled around on the chair.
For some reason, the air that night was breezy, unlike that of the previous nights, when it had been hot and stuffy. Madison opened the window a crack, sucked in a mouthful of night air, and kept typing.

Today I really paid attention to the wedding vows Dad and Stephanie read at the ceremony.

First of all they promised to have and hold. Then they promised to do it in good times and in bad times, in sickness and health, all the way until death. DEATH! What kind of a promise is that?

It sounds so morbid, but then I thought about it. There is nothing more romantic than forever, is there? Like, "I will love you forever and ever into infinity, my darling Madison." Just thinking about a boy saying that to me makes my head spin.

I can almost hear Hart's voice saying it. Almost.

Madison had just hit SAVE when she heard a knock at her door.

"Who is it?" she called out. The digital clock read nine-thirty. She guessed that maybe it was Tiffany. Madison's new cousin had promised to come by the room to hang out, since it was their last night together.

"Hello?" Madison called out, limping toward the door. Her ankle was still swollen from her fall. She leaned forward and peeped through the peephole. It was like peering into a teeny fish tank.

Dad and Stephanie stood there, all smiles, arm in arm.

"Maddie!" Dad said. He knocked again. "Open up, sweetie. It's us."

Madison quickly opened the door. "What are you guys doing here?" she asked. "Aren't you supposed to be at the ranch?"

Stephanie came into the room with her white dress trailing behind her. She kicked off her shoes and threw herself onto the bed.

"We escaped!" Stephanie said.

Madison's eyes darted from Dad to Stephanie and back to Dad again.

"Um . . ." Madison broke into a giggle. "Aren't you going to get in trouble or something?"

"Trouble?" Stephanie gasped. "You mean for leaving our own party?"

Dad laughed. "I'm all partied out, Maddie," he said.

"I totally agree," Stephanie said, rolling over onto her side. "And my mother can hunt us down and find us, but I don't think anyone's even noticed we left. Besides, we needed to see how you were feeling," Stephanie said.

"How's the ankle?" Dad asked.

Madison glanced down at the swelling. "It hurts. But I'll live."

"Thank goodness!" Stephanie said. "We were worried about you all night."

"You were? But it's your wedding day," Madison said. "Why were you worried about *me*?"

Stephanie made a face and sat up on the bed. "What a silly question," she said. "Now that I'm your

277

stepmother, you have to stop thinking like that. I am going to worry. All the time."

Madison felt herself blush. It felt strange to have someone besides Mom or Dad or even Gramma Helen say that kind of stuff.

"So, you've been on your laptop, I see," Dad said, looking over at Madison's computer.

She shot a look at the screen, but luckily her file had faded into a snow-leopard screen saver.

"I was just goofing around on bigfishbowl.com," Madison said.

"I hope you don't mind us dropping in on you," Stephanie said.

Madison shook her head. "Mind? No way. I'm happy. I feel honored."

Dad let out a belly laugh. "Honored? Oh, honey bear," he said, giving Madison a real bear hug. "I love you."

"I love you, too, Dad," Madison said. She felt a surge of emotion inside, as if all her worries from the weekend were washing onto some invisible shore. Everything had changed—but for the better? Dad and Stephanie were married, but they weren't running anywhere. . . . except here.

Madison looked over at the table in the room. On top, she spied the collage that she needed to give to Dad and Stephanie. Now was the time.

"Maddie?" Stephanie said. "Your father and I

wanted to thank you for all you did to make today truly special."

Madison shrugged. "You're welcome."

Stephanie turned to Dad with a funny nod, so Madison knew something was up.

"Do you want to do this?" Stephanie asked Dad.

He smiled. "No, you do it," Dad told Stephanie.

Out of her bag, Stephanie pulled out a perfectly wrapped pink box, tied in silver ribbon.

"This is for you," Stephanie said, handing Madison the box. "For everything you did to make our wedding the best day ever."

"A present?" she said. "For me?"

Dad beamed. "You deserve it," he said proudly. "You did such a good job with that reading. We were both very touched."

Madison looked down at the pink box and then shot a glance back over at her collage on the table.

"Um . . . before I open your box," Madison asked. "Can I give you guys *my* present, too?"

"Your present?" Stephanie said, looking very surprised. "What are you talking about?"

"Oh, Maddie, you didn't have to get us anything," Dad said.

"I didn't exactly *get* you something," Madison said. "Well . . . you'll see."

Madison pointed to the table where the collage was.

"Over there," she said, as Dad turned to look. "Happy Wedding."

Stephanie looked as if she'd been zapped with a stun gun. Dad froze, too.

"Aw, Maddie . . ." he started to say as Stephanie opened the outer envelope and they both saw the elaborate cover of the collage. He fell speechless.

Madison watched Stephanie put her head down and read the card from front to back without stopping. When she finally looked up, there were tears in her eyes.

For Dad and Stephanie

Your wedding is a special day
I'm sure you will be feeling good
  in every way
The sun is shining bright on your faces
Of course there is no one who can take
  your places
At first I thought this wedding would be
  weird
And that was just the start of what I feared
I know you're happy and I'm happy too
But I wondered what would happen with
  you two
And then I realized you will still be there
You will always listen and you will always care.
I know that sometimes I'm hard for Dad
  to take
Like when he says, "Maddie, give me a break."

Plus I have one mom and never had another

I'm not sure I know how to have a
  stepmother

I want our family to be complete and real

I want you both to know just how I feel.

You take care of me and let me share
  your life

Dad, I'm so glad you picked Stephanie for
  your wife

I hope that I will be a good part of the deal

I want you both to know just how I feel.

I wish you the best happy wedding time

Thanks for including me even though I can't
  really rhyme.

Love,

Madison

XOXOXOXOXOXO

Chapter 20

Stephanie blew her nose loudly. She couldn't stop crying.

"That—is—the—best—wedding—present—ever—" Stephanie gushed.

Dad rubbed his new wife's back.

"Take a deep breath, Steph," he said, winking at Madison. "I'm amazed you have any tears left after this week."

"Me, too," Madison said awkwardly.

"Oh, Maddie!" Stephanie cried. "I never expected anything! You know that—"

"I know," Madison said. "But the unexpected things are the best kinds of presents, though, right? That's what my Gramma says. . . ."

"*You*'re the best present," Stephanie said, wiping

her face. She leaned over to hug Madison and then excused herself and disappeared into the bathroom.

Dad planted a loud smooch on Madison's cheek. "You're something else," he said, shaking his head. "You never cease to amaze me."

Madison gave Dad a kiss right back. "I really am happy now, Dad," she admitted. "Happier than happy. Isn't that funny?"

Stephanie came back out of the bathroom with renewed energy.

"Well," Stephanie said, clearing her throat. "I know it can't compare to your beautiful gift, Madison. But please open our special present next?"

Madison looked over at the pink box. She'd nearly forgotten. The wrapping paper was sealed with little gold wafer stickers. Madison knew it was from some fancy shop. She guessed it was jewelry because of its size.

The box inside the paper wrapping was silver. Madison lifted the lid and gasped.

Inside the box was a necklace with a heart-charm locket.

"Look close," Dad said. "Real close."

Madison examined the charm and opened the locket. Inside was a teeny photo of Dad, Madison, and Stephanie.

"This is a picture from that trip we took," Madison said as she peered at the locket. "I remember this. We're all laughing."

Dad smiled. "Exactly. Remember when we took it? We were up by Lake Dora."

Madison turned to Dad and Stephanie, her mouth open in astonishment. "I love it," she said, her lips quivering a little in surprise at the intensity of her own reaction. She stared back down at the necklace and sighed. "I love you guys so much," Madison said.

Stephanie and Dad reached out for her at the same time.

It was their first official "family" hug.

After the exchange of gifts, Dad and Stephanie said good night and headed in to the room next door. Even though it was already later than late, and Madison was still laid up, Dad gave her special permission to have Tiffany and a few of the other cousins come up to the hotel room to rent a movie and get room service if they liked. Her new cousins even had permission to crash on the floor for the night.

Since Tiffany and the others took their time getting up to the hotel room, Madison took advantage of the wait to get back online and check her e-mailbox.

FROM	SUBJECT
✉ Bigwheels	Whats Going On
✉ ff_budgefilms	How was the wedding?

Bigwheels wrote to say that she was worried because Madison hadn't written in the last twenty-four hours—and she wanted more wedding updates. Madison shot her a quick e-mail right back.

From: MadFinn
To: Bigwheels
Subject: Re: Whats Going On
Date: Sat 20 July 10:18 PM

Sorry for being outta touch. You won't believe how this weekend has turned out. I don't think I even believe it. Dad and Stephanie seem so happy and I am too. At least that's what I told my dad. I'm still a little freaked, but they're being so nice to me. Everyone is. And get this. I am about to have my very own slumber party right here in the middle of Texas with girls I thought would never even TALK to me let alone sleep on my floor!

The wedding service was beautiful. I couldn't stop sweating when I did my reading, but I don't think anyone noticed. Luckily no one was standing behind me or staring at my armpits. Thanks again for all ur cool advice.

p.s. I got along great with my new cousins Kirk and Tiffany after all. And even though Kirk is like the cutest boy I have ever seen (no exaggeration THE cutest), he is now more than Stephanie's nephew he's my cousin so I have decided that is too bizarre to crush on him. What do you think? Besides, I've been obsessing about Hart again for some reason. I even had a dream about him last night! He was riding in this carriage and carrying flowers and candles. Don't ask.

I still have to give you the play by play of everything that happened, but I'll write more 18r when we fly home tomorrow, ok? Write back 2 me.

Yours till the cup cakes,

Maddie

The next message was from Mom. It was short and sweet.
I miss you. How are you? Where are you?
Madison thought about calling Mom back, but decided that she didn't want to risk waking her up in the middle of the night for the second or third time

that weekend. So she clicked REPLY to send an e-mail instead.

From: MadFinn
To: ff__budgefilms
Subject: Re: How was the wedding?
Date: Sat 20 July 10:27 PM

Mom I think ur in bed so I wont
call u now. We just this second got
back to the hotel and the wedding
was GREAT just like you said it
would be. (Thanks for calming me
down.) Tonite I gave Stephanie and
Dad my present and they were
totally psyched. I want u 2 know
that I miss u and can't wait to
come home 2 u and Phinnie tomorrow.

p.s. I fell tonight and sprained my
ankle a little but it is ok now I
think. Dad took good care of me.
I'll tell u more l8r.

p.p.s. I love u lots

Madison clicked SEND. Her computer beeped. She punched a few different keys. All at once, an Insta-Message appeared.

<Balletgrl>: Maddie is that YOU?????

Madison couldn't believe her luck. Even though it had to be midnight back in Far Hills, Aimee was online.

<MadFinn>: I can't believe ur here
<Balletgrl>: me neither this is the coolest
<MadFinn>: but it's sooo late
<Balletgrl>: I know but its Saturday and Billy was on the computr b4 and I really wanted to check out bigfishbowl tonite they had free games my mom and dad aren't awake
<MadFinn>: I MISS YOOOOOO AIM
<Balletgrl>: when r u coming back???
<MadFinn>: tomorrrrrrrow AM
<Balletgrl>: the wedding wuz 2day right?
<MadFinn>: yup--and I fell and totally twisted my ankle when my dad asked me 2 dance how dumb is that?
<Balletgrl>: no way
<MadFinn>: everything was so nice though and my cousins r all being super nice 2 me
<Balletgrl>: :>)
<MadFinn>: how r things there? How is FIONA
<Balletgrl>: OMG she is good--and so is her dad they released him fm

Intensive Care and now he's in a regular hospital room he will go home 18r this wk isn't that the BEST NEWS EVER?

\<MadFinn\>: I am so glad

\<Balletgrl\>: I skipped dance & spent this morning @ the hospital w/her which was a good thing she's kinda sad you'll see when u get back

\<MadFinn\>: ur a good friend Aim

\<Balletgrl\>: u would have done the same thing 4 me

\<MadFinn\>: I feel so bad not being there!

\<Balletgrl\>: stop worrying you'll be here in less than a day no prob

\<MadFinn\>: IK ur right

\<Balletgrl\>: BTW I have something else really weird to tell u--REALLY WEIRD

\<MadFinn\>: what?

\<Balletgrl\>: today I went over 2 the bookstore after the hospital b/c my dad needed help

\<MadFinn\>: yeah

\<Balletgrl\>: So, I saw Hart there

\<MadFinn\>: Hart Jones?

\<Balletgrl\>: he was looking for some summr rdg book or something

\<MadFinn\>: so?

\<Balletgrl\>: n e way he asked how u were

\<MadFinn\>: huh?

\<Balletgrl\>: I didn't really think about it much but then he asked again "so how is Madison?" like he missed seeing u or something I don't know how to explain it he was too curious d' you know what I mean???

\<MadFinn\>: that is weird I guess hmmmm

\<Balletgrl\>: SO?

\<MadFinn\>: So what?

\<Balletgrl\>: SO do u like him? Tell me the TRUTH something is definitely up

\<MadFinn\>: what do u mean?

\<Balletgrl\>: u always ask about him 2 admit it

\<MadFinn\>: no I don't

\<Balletgrl\>: don't lie 2 me I'm ur BFF and I know

\<MadFinn\>: I think Hart is nice

\<Balletgrl\>: How nice?

\<MadFinn\>: Nice nice. I dunno.

\<Balletgrl\>: Oh wow u totally DO like him I can't believe I never noticed this b4 I've been living on another planet OMG!!!!!

\<MadFinn\>: Aimee ur crazy

```
<Balletgrl>: AND U R SUCH A LIAR
<MadFinn>: I am not!!!!!
<Balletgrl>: Fiona is going to DIE
   when she hears this
<MadFinn>: hears what I haven't said
   n e thing Aim
<Balletgrl>: Maddie, u r so busted
```

Madison held her breath. The truth was out. She didn't know how to lie anymore about her feelings for Hart—but she couldn't talk about him, either.

And how was she supposed to feel about Aimee's news that Hart was asking about *her*?

```
<Balletgrl>: r u still there or
   what
```

Madison's fingers stroked the keys absently. She didn't know what else to say. Lie or deny? Ultimately, Madison did what she did best.

She ran away.

```
<MadFinn>: um . . . Aim I have 2 go
   my dad is @ the door
<Balletgrl>: no he is not
<MadFinn>: yeah he is so and I have
   2 go I'll call u when I get back
   tell Fiona hello ok?
<Balletgrl>: I'm telling her MORE
   than that, Maddie LOL
```

```
<MadFinn>: ok whatever gotta run bye
<Balletgrl>: C U
```

As soon as Madison clicked offline, there was a knock at her door. Tiffany arrived with her two cousins Rebecca and Lynne.

"Sorry we took so long!" Tiffany said as Madison opened the door. "My mother wanted to give me a million rules about what I could and couldn't do, and finally she just let us go."

"Hi," Rebecca and Lynne said at the same time.

Tiffany did the rest of the talking.

"These are your cousins, too, but I'm first and they're second cousins. Something like that, I think. Anyway, what are we doing just standing here? We have to order ice cream from room service and we have to watch a movie. We can watch an *R* movie, too, because our parents are not here. This is so great."

Madison smiled. "Thanks for coming. It's nice to have the company."

Tiffany smiled right back. "As far as I'm concerned, getting to know you is the best part of the whole wedding. Kirk said the same thing."

"Really?" Madison asked.

"Of course! Our family is always the same people, over and over," Tiffany explained. "You are so much more fun."

Madison didn't think that she was any fun at all,

especially considering the fact that she had been lame (for real!) during most of the wedding reception. She hobbled over to the bed to clear off some of her things.

Tiffany, of course, didn't need an invitation to sit down. She went right over and leaped onto the bed. Rebecca and Lynne followed her.

"Okay! What should we order from room service?" Tiffany asked as she opened up one of the gold-colored menus. "I'm not hungry, but we have to order something."

Madison collapsed into the chair by the table and shrugged. "Order whatever you want. My dad says it's his treat," she said.

As Tiffany, Rebecca, and Lynne read the room service menu from cover to cover, Madison started thinking about Hart again.

Was *real* love waiting for Madison back home in Far Hills?

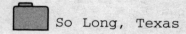 So Long, Texas

So we're on the plane now. Going home at
last. And my ankle is feeling way better,
too. My foot actually fit into my sandal
this morning.

Dad, Stephanie, Uncle Rick, Aunt Violet,
and I went to this HUGE breakfast back at
Wolfe Ranch this morning with eggs and
steak and way too much food for the
amount of people there. After that we said
good-bye and Mrs. Wolfe drove us all to the
Houston airport in this minivan. After
everything that happened this weekend I
thought Stephanie would act weird toward

her mom, but she didn't. She was bawling her eyes out in the car like she was SAD to go. Mrs. Wolfe was acting sad, too.

Is that how it works with parents? They make you crazy and then you love them more?

Rude Awakening: I hope that life isn't one big joke because I sometimes I just don't get it.

Dad says they decided not to take a big honeymoon right away because Stephanie has some work deal. They are going to Paris or someplace super romantic eventually. Maybe in the fall, Dad says. After the wedding, I feel like they're the celebrities of the weekend or something. But I'm the luckiest because I get them all to myself today.

Kirk and Tiffany were nicer than nice to me this morning. Kirk asked me to write and Tiff (she said I should call her that from now on) gave me her e-mail even though she claims she has no idea how to use a computer and made me promise I would write. She gave me her cell phone number too, just in case. I can't believe she has her own cell phone and her own line in her bedroom, too. Mom would never let me have that. Would she?

I am so glad to have new cousins like them. I guess I was a little harsh when I first met them but whatever. I wonder what they really thought of me?

The best news of going home OF COURSE is that I get to see Fiona for the first time since everything happened w/her dad. I was really worried for a while. I just can't help but think what if something worse had happened? What would Fiona do? Gramma Helen always says it's better not to worry about things you can't control. I guess she's right. I have to stop worrying about stuff so much.

"The plane is starting its descent," Dad said, reaching over Stephanie to tap Madison on the knee.

Madison jumped, startled. She'd been so busy writing on her laptop for a good part of the flight that she'd practically forgotten where she was.

"We're already home?" Madison asked. She glanced out the airplane window and saw land.

"Almost," Dad said. "We have about a half hour more, I think."

Stephanie leaned over Madison's shoulder. "I think we're over Maryland or Pennsylvania somewhere," she said. "Look at all of those farms."

Madison glanced out the window for farms, but all she saw were houses after houses in developments that speckled the landscape. It was hard to believe that so many people lived all crammed in together down there. Madison wondered what her Far Hills neighborhood looked like from the sky.

"Can I see your ring again?" Madison asked Stephanie, who held it out proudly.

The diamonds on Stephanie's wedding band glimmered in the dull light inside the plane.

297

Madison was impressed that Dad had selected the band all by himself. He said Stephanie had given him some hints, so he had known what to buy, but Madison knew he was just being nice and giving her the credit.

The more time she spent with the two of them, Madison saw how happy and perfectly they fit together. Maybe better than Dad and Mom had ever fit? It was a strange thing to consider.

"I'm glad we're all flying home together," Dad said as the plane banked to the left. Madison felt her body shift toward the window. The FASTEN SEAT BELTS sign went on.

"We're flying home together like a real family," Stephanie said, quickly adding, "Your *second* family, of course."

Madison smiled. Maybe Stephanie wasn't trying to take Mom's place. Maybe she was just trying to be nice.

The plane landed, and everyone on board applauded, including Madison. They exited the plane and headed straight for the baggage-claim area.

When Madison spotted the luggage already spinning around on the carousel in the baggage claim area, she let out a chant: "No more lost bags! No more lost bags!"

She spotted her checkered suitcase as soon as it appeared on the conveyor belt.

"Dad!" Madison cried, pointing to the bag.

He laughed and helped her lift the suitcase onto a cart. After a few minutes, Stephanie's and Dad's suitcases also appeared. Madison and her dad and Stephanie headed for the exit. As they emerged from the building, Madison saw a sign that read *FINN*. A gentleman in a suit stood in front of a black, stretch limousine.

"What's this?" Stephanie asked when she saw the sign.

Dad grinned. "A surprise."

"A limo!" Madison shouted. She ran to the door and looked through the car window. "There's a T.V. inside. Wow! Dad, this is awesome."

The three climbed into the back while the limousine driver placed their luggage into the trunk.

"First stop, Blueberry Street!" Madison joked. She sat back in a leather comfy seat facing Dad and Stephanie.

"This is very sweet, Jeff," Stephanie said grinning. "Really."

"Sweets for *my* two sweets," Dad joked, kissing Stephanie on the forehead and blowing a kiss in Madison's direction.

"Oh, gag me, Dad," Madison said, pinching her nose. "I thought that getting married would make you *less* sappy."

"Not likely," Dad said with a shrug.

The limo pulled out of the airport and headed for downtown Far Hills. There was a lot of traffic, so

299

some roads were slow going, but eventually the new family made its way to Madison's and Mom's house.

"Look who's waiting for you," Dad said as they pulled up into the driveway.

"Phinnie!" Madison shouted. "And Aimee and Blossom!"

It was like a Welcome Home committee.

"Maddie," Stephanie said, grabbing Madison's wrist before Madison could get out of the limo. "Thanks again—for everything. . . ."

"You're welcome," Madison said.

But Stephanie still didn't let go of her. In fact, she squeezed harder. "I just want you to know, Maddie, that I will treasure that collage and poem forever. I know how much you mean to your dad and . . ."

"Stephanie," Madison said. "You're going to cry again, aren't you?"

Dad let out a little laugh. "She's got your number, Steph," he said.

Stephanie held back her sniffles. "I guess so," she said with a smile. "Go on and get out of the car!"

Madison wasn't quite sure how to say good-bye to her new stepmother, so she just threw herself forward and landed a kiss on Stephanie's cheek.

"See you later," Madison mumbled. She fingered the charm necklace that she'd worn all the way from Texas. "Thanks for this, too."

"Let me help the driver get your bags," Dad said, hopping out of the car.

Madison slung her orange bag over one shoulder and slid out of the car. She hurried up the walkway to the house with her arms open wide.

"Phinnie!" Madison shouted. The pug raced down the walkway toward her and began to paw Madison's shins, panting wildly.

"Oh, my goodness, I am soooo glad you're home!" Aimee called out, racing down the path herself, with Blossom in tow.

"Rowwrrrorooooo!" both dogs howled in stereo.

Dad took the suitcase up to the house. Mom was standing in the doorway. Madison saw them exchange a few words. Mom stood at the screen door and waved to the limousine.

At first, Madison thought Mom was waving at *her*, but then she realized that the wave meant for Stephanie.

"Congratulations," Mom cried.

Stephanie poked her head out of the limousine window. "Thanks, Fran," she said.

Dad and Mom were both smiling, so Madison knew everything was okay—at least as okay as it would ever be. The two of them weren't ever going to be reuniting. That was that.

Madison dropped her orange bag and bent down to cuddle Phinnie in her arms. "Oh, I missed you so much," she cooed in his ear. "My Phinnie!"

"Wait a sec! Do you have a tan?" Aimee said, sounding envious.

"A tan! Are you crazy?" Madison asked.

Dad ambled back down the walkway, all smiles.

"Congrats, Mr. Finn," Aimee said. She was in constant motion, as usual.

"Thanks, Aimee," Dad said. "And now, my dear Madison, I must bid you adieu."

"Oh, Dad," Madison said. "Cut it out!"

"This is only good-bye for now," he said, wrapping his arm around Madison. "Until we meet again?"

"Dad!" Madison wriggled out of his grip. "Stop being so goofy." She rolled her eyes. "Dad, you are so embarrassing. And I am crowning you King of the Dumb Jokes. It's official."

"What happened to King of the Sappy Moments?" he asked.

"Oh, Dad. Just *go*!" Madison said, pushing him back toward the limo.

"I'll talk to you later," Dad said as he climbed back into the car. The limo pulled away with a toot of the horn. Madison and Aimee waved.

From the porch, Mom called out to Madison. "Welcome back!"

Madison turned and headed up onto the porch for a welcome-home hug from Mom.

"You look surprisingly rested for someone who barely slept all weekend," Mom said. "Let me see that twisted ankle. Your dad says you are feeling better."

Madison and Mom sat on the porch steps together.

Aimee came over and joined them, while the dogs played on the lawn. Madison recounted all the wedding details she could recall, from the layout of Wolfe ranch to the view from Bobcat Lake. She told them about the ice sculpture shaped like Texas and about the relative with the big, pink hair.

"Fiona is going to love hearing about that one!" Aimee said.

"Where's Fiona right now?" Madison asked.

"Home with her dad and everyone else in her family," Aimee explained. "She wanted to come over and say hello to you, but her mom needed her help. I told her we'd go over there, but her mom isn't really up for visitors tonight. She said we should come by tomorrow, instead."

"Sounds good," Madison said.

"She said to tell you not to forget to bring your plane letter!" Aimee said.

"Oh, wow. I almost forgot!" Madison cried. She went over to her orange bag and pulled out the answers to her questions from the plane. She and Aimee collapsed onto the couch and read the answers together.

Midway through, Aimee started to chuckle.

"What's so funny?" Madison asked.

"I told Fiona what you said about Hart," Aimee said.

"You *what*?" Madison cried. "Aim! I didn't say anything!"

"That is big news. It isn't fair to keep that a secret from your BFFs. Anyway, what's so bad about liking Hart Jones? He's cute."

"What's this I hear about Hart?" Mom asked, appearing from the kitchen.

Madison hung her head in her hands. Now Mom had to know, too? She didn't know what to say. Aimee, as usual, filled in the blanks.

"Maddie likes Hart," Aimee said. "He's this kid in our class. . . ."

"Really?" Mom said, looking very surprised. "I thought you liked that boy Drew."

"Drew? You do?" Aimee said, shocked.

"*Mom!*" Madison yelled. "What are you talking about? I never . . . ever . . . *ever* said that I liked Drew."

"Oh, really? Was it Dan, then? I can't remember," Mom said.

"Pork-O?" Aimee shouted.

"*Mom!*" Madison cried. She curled up in a ball on the sofa.

"How long have you liked Dan, Maddie?" Aimee cried. "Wow. You never said anything. I mean, we all know Dan likes *you*, but . . ."

"Huh?" Madison cried. "What are you talking about?"

Mom chuckled. "Sounds to me like you have nothing to worry about, Maddie."

Madison was sure she'd turned four successive

shades of red by then. "I think you have both lost your minds!" she exclaimed, slowly getting up off the couch.

Phin followed Madison into the kitchen. Mom and Aimee came, too, but luckily, the subject changed back from boys to the wedding.

Over dinner, Madison regaled everyone with more stories of Tiffany, tuxedos, and everything Texas. Before they knew it, the meal was over, the dishes were washed, and it was time for Aimee to head home again with Blossom. She made no more mention of Hart or Drew or Dan or anyone else.

Whew, thought Maddie.

"Maddie, you have to call me first thing in the morning," Aimee said. "We'll go over to Fiona's together, 'kay?"

"Okay," Madison said. She hugged her friend good night. "I'm so glad to see you, Aim."

"That goes double for me," Aimee said, giving Madison a big hug back. "Bye, Mrs. Finn!"

Madison's mom waved a dish towel at the girls from the kitchen. "Good night, Aimee."

The dogs said their own good-byes. They always sniffed each other or rubbed noses before parting ways.

As Madison closed the screen door and watched her friend disappear down the block, she looked up at the big, round moon in the sky over Far Hills. It was the same moon that she'd seen just one night before over Bobcat Lake. But this moon seemed very different. Everything about Texas and the wedding seemed far away. Madison wondered if she would really keep in touch with Kirk or Tiffany or any of the cousins she'd met in Bellville.

Slowly, Madison turned and limped back into the house. Mom agreed to walk Phin before bed, so Madison said good night and hobbled up to her room, laptop in hand.

Madison booted up the computer, logged on, and opened her e-mailbox. She typed in Bigwheels's e-mail address.

From: MadFinn
To: Bigwheels
Subject: back home
Date: Sun 21 July 8:48 PM

I know I only wrote yesterday, but I'm back @ home now and I just wanted to see if maybe u were online but ur not so I'll send email instead.

Wow. I feel like SUCH a different person since we took this trip. At the wedding, Dad & Stephanie were the ones who made this big promise to have and to hold each other until infinity. But when I was in

Texas I realized that I have a lot
to hold onto, too.

Of course I have BFFs like Aim and
Fiona. And I have my mom, my dad,
and now a stepmother, too. BTW: Do
u think 3 parents r better than 2?
I'm not 100% sure yet.

Do u ever look up in the sky b4 u
go to sleep? There is this huge
white ball of a moon up there
tonight. I should write a poem
about it. I bet u would. Isn't it
cool that that same moon is hanging
over Texas where I just visited AND
it's also hanging over your house,
too? Do u see it?

I guess I was afraid that
everything would change if Dad got
married again. Like I thought I
would lose him. But I guess I
haven't lost n e thing. Except my
mind. LOL.

Oh--there is some BIG newz I forgot
to mention. Aim & Fiona know about
Hart now. So I guess I did lose one
thing--the secretive part of my
secret crush. I don't know what

will happen now that he's sure to
find out how I feel. Cross ur
fingers that he likes me back.

Write sooner than soon?

Yours till the friend ships,

Maddie

p.s. I almost 4got 2 say THANKS
again. It's nice knowing I can have
and hold onto YOU too. SLFN!

Mad Chat Words:

```
o:-\              Pea brain
:-{}              Blowing a kiss
(:-<              Feeling worried
HAGT              Have a good time
WAM               Wait a minute
TTYT              Talk to you tomorrow
SSS               Sorry so short
BION              Believe it or not
L8ly              Lately
OCN               Of course not
KIR               Keep it real
WAYTA?            What are you talking about?
YR                Yeah, right
ILYG              I love you guys
VB                Volleyball
SLFN!             So long for now!
Sez               says
```

Madison's Computer Tip

I have decided that traveling makes e-mail the Number One essential thing on the planet. I don't know WHAT I would have done if I couldn't have e-mailed Bigwheels and all my friends in Far Hills when I went to Dad's and Stephanie's wedding! And I never would have gotten Aimee's e-mail about Fiona's Dad, either. Plus, the computer is a great way to keep track of everything that happens when you go away. **Use a laptop to keep a travel diary.** I wrote down all the things that happened at the wedding—even the not-so-fun stuff. But I'm glad I did. Now I can remember Dad's second wedding for always. Once again, the files of Madison Finn (AKA little old me) came in handy.

Visit Madison at www.madisonfinn.com